MURDER MOST FOWL

A WILDWOOD WITCH MYSTERY: BOOK 2

ELLE ADAMS

This book was written, produced and edited in the UK, where some spelling, grammar and word usage will vary from US English.

Copyright © 2021 Elle Adams
All rights reserved.

To be notified when Elle Adams's next book is released, sign up to her author newsletter.

My first day as Head Witch began with my new "co-worker" hacking up a hair ball on my desk.

"Thanks for that, Carmilla." I shooed my late grandmother's ancient cat off the desk before she made a mess of the considerable number of papers stacked on top of the wooden surface. I'd already had to move them away from my squirrel familiar, Tansy, as she ran up and down the room, inspecting the various shelves and cabinets.

"You're welcome," Carmilla said. "I thought I'd make you feel at home in your new office."

At least she was acknowledging it was mine, which was an improvement, but I hadn't quite dared to start rearranging the office to my liking. Mostly because the previous owner wasn't quite gone yet. Grandma's ghost hovered in the corner, casting a critical eye over the dusty cloak I'd had to dig out of the back of my wardrobe and the socks depicting cartoon squirrels I wore underneath.

I expected a lecture on inappropriate office attire, but

instead, Grandma asked, "*What* have you done with that sceptre?"

"You said to keep it within reach." I indicated the long polished instrument, which I'd rested against the back of the desk next to my knees. Part of my new job as Head Witch involved carrying the sceptre wherever I went, but it was difficult to fit a long pointed stick in my pocket or up my sleeve like my wand.

"The disrespect." She huffed. "Have you even tried using it to cast a spell yet?"

"I haven't had time." I'd been given a grand total of one day to prepare for my new job, and I'd spent most of it tying up loose ends with my former employer. Telling the head of the magical courier company I worked for that I'd be taking a year-long hiatus because I'd unexpectedly been chosen as the regional Head Witch had gone over like a lead broomstick. I had an inkling there wouldn't *be* a job for me to return to once my time as Head Witch came to an end, but that was assuming I survived the first day. Carmilla, for one, seemed convinced that I wouldn't last a week.

"Well, make time," said the ancient cat. "You can't protect yourself from assassins if you don't learn to use the sceptre."

"What assassins?" My own Aunt Shannon had tried to claim the sceptre as her own, and in trying to keep her hands off it, I'd accidentally claimed it as my own in the process. Or rather, the other way around, since the sceptre chose its wielder using a kind of magic which was mystifying to everyone. Even my grandmother, who'd held the title for several decades until her untimely death a couple of weeks ago, hadn't known that I'd be expected to step directly into her shoes without a clue as to why the sceptre had picked the family screwup as its wielder.

"Do you have any idea how many assassination attempts I fought off over the years?" Grandma's ghost asked me. "Always be on your guard."

"I would if I knew what I was supposed to be on my guard for. Except collapsing piles of paperwork maybe."

Grandma hadn't been exactly untidy, but her office contained far more cabinets full of papers than one would reasonably expect to fit into such a small space. I'd better hope I never needed to access anything from the very back of the room because I couldn't even see the wall behind the mass of filing cabinets and bookshelves, including the large store of ingredients for spells and potions. Meanwhile, my desk had drawers hidden in every nook and cranny, for most of which I had no idea where to find the keys.

"Don't be flippant," Carmilla chastised me. "And do keep that familiar of yours under control."

Tansy leapt down from the top of a cabinet in a rustle of papers, scampering over to the desk.

"I'm not being flippant. I'm being practical," I said. "Doesn't the sceptre automatically shoot bolts of purple light at people who threaten me? I think that'd be enough to deter most assassins."

Otherwise, it was supposed to work the same as a regular wand, albeit a larger more unwieldy one. At least Grandma seemed to have finally given up on trying to reclaim it for her own, as ghosts found it hard to make contact with any solid objects, and her attempts to pick up the sceptre had ended in failure.

"Not all of them," said Grandma. "They're sneaky. You

need to take precautions to check your food for poison or stop eating out altogether."

"Oh, come on." While Mum did employ a cook at home—a necessity, given that none of my family members had any culinary skills to speak of—my occasional evening meals at the Fox's Den with my best friend, Piper, were one of the only "normal" things I might be able to keep in my life. Also, I'd draw the line at giving up my lattes from Were's My Coffee?, the shifter-run café above which my cousin Rowan was now living.

Admittedly, Grandma had been poisoned by her own assistant—by accident—and she had good reason to be paranoid that someone would try to take me out of the picture before my term as Head Witch officially began. Still, hiding away wasn't my style.

"Also, you need to keep an eye on that sceptre at all times," added Carmilla.

"If I have to carry it everywhere, it's not like it'll leave my sight." Since everyone knew my family, I'd never exactly been anonymous, but I didn't look forward to the extra attention I'd draw while walking around town carrying a giant pointed instrument with a glowing purple gem on its end. While stealing the Head Witch's sceptre was a foolish idea at best, it wasn't unheard of, and certain members of my family had been willing to try anything to win it over. Though I'd definitively beaten them, I doubted they'd entirely given up on their goals yet. For that reason, I'd put up with the stares I'd attract by wielding the sceptre in public.

"Do you know what happened to my predecessor?" Grandma asked.

"No." Even Mum hadn't been born yet when Grandma

had first taken the title of Head Witch. "Was she assassinated?"

She drifted alongside the desk. "We think so."

"That's not very specific," I said. "How'd she die?"

"She choked on a sunflower seed."

"That doesn't sound like an assassination to me, Grandma."

"Your risk to take."

Carmilla hopped over to the other side of the desk, knocking a container of pens over in the process.

Honestly. Between her and Grandma, I'd be lucky to get any actual work done before anyone had the chance to threaten my life. Figuring I might as well seize the chance to test the sceptre, I lifted it into the air and cast a levitation charm to move the fallen pens back into the container.

The pens shot straight up into the air and so did several stacks of papers on the desk. Not to mention Carmilla, who gave an outraged yowl, her paws flailing in midair. "Put me down!"

"Sorry!" I hastened to undo the spell, causing everything to come crashing back to earth. Carmilla landed in a pile of papers, puncturing them with her claws, and then sprinted over to hide behind Grandma's ghost.

"You," said Grandma, "are a menace."

I gave the sceptre a sheepish look. "I didn't know it'd be that strong."

"It's a sceptre, not a party trick."

"You told me it was the same as a wand." I climbed out of my chair to collect the fallen papers, most of which were written in Grandma's scrawling, semi-legible handwriting.

"I've changed my mind," said Grandma. "You're welcome to treat it like an ornamental stick if it keeps you out of trouble."

I opted not to dignify that with a response, instead getting down on hands and knees to retrieve all the pens and papers which had fallen onto the floor. Didn't she have digital copies of anything? Given my family's proclivity for living in the past, I guessed not. Not all covens had upgraded to the modern age, and I didn't even see a computer anywhere amid the stacked cabinets.

This is going to be trickier than I thought.

I hadn't exactly come into the position of Head Witch expecting an easy ride. I'd already been braced for the naysayers who believed the nonsense that the *Blue Moon* tabloid printed about my family on a daily basis. I made a point of ignoring the headlines, but that didn't stop the weight of my family's expectations from resting heavily on my shoulders—both the living family members and the dead ones.

I laid the last paper on top of the heap on the desk. "What's on the agenda for today? I'm meeting with the council representatives of the Wildwood Coven, aren't I?"

"In an hour," said Grandma. "Also, you *are* a council representative, technically speaking."

"More of a ceremonial one."

As the new leader of the Wildwood Coven, my mother was the driving force behind the witches who ran the town of Wildwood Heath. The role of Head Witch was mostly to act as a judge on matters affecting all the local covens, not just the Wildwood witches, but Grandma had held both titles, and Mum had expected to follow in her footsteps.

Instead, the sceptre had chosen me, with the result that I'd have to spend the next year travelling to meetings with both the local covens and the regional ones and settling various disputes. That would have been tricky enough to handle if I'd stayed local, but in the last few years, I'd spent more time away from Wildwood Heath than not, and I hadn't exactly stayed up to date on the goings-on in the covens in the interim.

Someone rapped on the office door, interrupting my thoughts.

"There she is," said Grandma.

"There who is?" I rose to my feet and called out, "Come in!"

A young witch ambled into the room, dressed in the customary long black coat of a council member and with her long curly dark hair tied in a ponytail. To my utter bafflement, she dropped into a curtsy, deep enough that her glasses almost fell off the end of her nose. "Head Witch. It's an honour to meet you."

"Er... you can just call me Robin," I said. "Also, there's no need for... that." I gestured at her hunched position, and she straightened upright at once. "Can I help you?"

"I..." She glanced over her shoulder. "I'm Chloe Watts, your new assistant. I thought you knew."

"Who...?" *Mum.* It was just like her to hire me an assistant without asking my permission first.

"Good, you're here," said Grandma. "Chloe, bring Robin her correspondence."

"My what?" I said blankly.

Chloe raised her wand and gave it a wave. The papers on the desk shifted to make room for another heap of what appeared to be letters.

"What are these?" I peered at the spiky handwriting on the topmost piece of paper. *Dear Head Witch,* it began.

"Letters from the other Head Witches congratulating you on your position," said Grandma. "It's courteous to write back, thanking all of them."

"Write back." My gaze skimmed across the letters, of which there were at least two dozen. "You mean now?"

"Yes," said Carmilla with a barely concealed laugh. "You don't want to give a bad impression to your fellow Head Witches, do you?"

"Not at all." I turned to Grandma's ghost. "Do you happen to have a computer somewhere in here?"

Tansy popped up. "In the desk. Bottom drawer on the right. I checked."

"Don't touch that," Grandma reprimanded when I opened the drawer to reveal a rather dusty laptop.

Carmilla sauntered over and flicked the drawer shut with her tail. "Write back by hand."

"You've got to be joking." It'd take all morning to reply to all of them, and my handwriting was more or less illegible even if you didn't take my difficulties with spelling into account. The nonmagical type of spelling, that is. In the normal world, they called it dyslexia or something similar. While I did know a handy spellchecker charm, writing fifty letters by hand did not strike me as a productive use of my time.

"Sorry," Chloe said. "It's customary. Right, Head Witch —ah, I mean... Mrs Wildwood?"

I looked at her in bafflement for a moment until I realised she was addressing Grandma's ghost. She'd gone by Head Witch for so long that I sometimes forgot her actual name.

"Precisely," said Grandma.

"Maybe it was the custom when you became Head Witch, but computers didn't exist then," I pointed out, picking up one of the letters. "Look, some of these are typed, not handwritten."

Grandma drifted behind me, stirring up a breeze that caused the letter to fly out of my hand and land back on top of the pile. "It doesn't interest me what the *other* Head Witches do. We have our traditions."

"Including giving ourselves hand cramps and living in a forest of paperwork?" I could see how she'd amassed so many cabinets of files over the years. "Chloe, do all the Head Witches write personalised responses to every letter?"

She shifted from one foot to another. "I don't think so, but I'm not privy to how the other Head Witches run things."

"Don't you start pressuring her," Carmilla reprimanded me. "Having an assistant isn't an excuse not to do anything yourself."

"That isn't the plan." I felt sorry for Chloe, since I doubted that she'd known what she was getting into when she'd applied for the job, but I was pretty sure this was exactly the kind of task I was supposed to give to my assistant. There must be a magical shortcut to writing fifty-odd letters.

I drew in a breath and faced Grandma. "Would it be acceptable if I wrote a standard letter and then used a copying charm to make fifty duplicates before adding in the right names and titles afterwards?"

"If you can use a copying charm correctly, then of

course," said Grandma. "I seem to remember that wasn't one of your strong points."

You didn't have to remind me. Unfortunately, the last time I'd tried that charm, I'd accidentally created a reflection of the text which nobody could read without holding it up to a mirror. Then again, I wasn't the only person here capable of using magic. "Chloe, can you cast an adequate copying spell?"

"Of course," Chloe said. "I'll gladly help you."

Maybe there was something to having an assistant after all, though I had the suspicion I wouldn't be able to send her to attend tedious three-hour meetings in my place. Ah well. "Thanks. Where's the blank paper?"

"In there." She waved her wand, and a cabinet door swung open behind me. "Is there anything else you need me to do?"

"Can you check if there's anything else urgent on the agenda for the day? I have to head to a meeting in less than an hour."

"I can give you a list," said Grandma.

"You didn't tell *me* that." I did my best to swallow down my annoyance, but Grandma probably knew Chloe much better than I did. "Can the two of you talk between yourselves while I write the letter, please?"

"Only because you asked so nicely." Grandma drifted over to Chloe, who looked surprisingly unbothered at the notion of dealing with the ghost of my predecessor. Grandma's own assistant had landed in jail for murder, so hiring a replacement hadn't exactly been at the top of my never-ending to-do list.

"If you don't finish before the council meeting, you can take the letters home and finish them this evening," added Carmilla. "They need to be mailed out before tomorrow."

"Noted." I selected a piece of parchment, trying to ignore Carmilla's expectant stare. I'd come in here determined to do a good job despite not being prepared for the position, but my family and I tended not to align with the same views on… well, anything.

I wrote my response slowly and carefully, copying the formal tone of the congratulatory letters and doing my best to avoid using any words I wasn't sure how to spell. My wrist had cramped by the time I'd finished, but I didn't think I'd made any heinous mistakes.

"You missed out an 'i,'" said Grandma.

"Thanks." I gingerly corrected the word, holding my hand as steady as possible to avoid having to rewrite the whole thing again. Then I pulled out my wand to cast a spellchecker charm, not quite trusting the sceptre after the mishap with the levitation spell earlier. Nothing lit up in red, so I didn't have any more errors to fix. *Good.*

Chloe sprang over to the desk. "Need me to cast the spell?"

"Yes, please." I handed her the piece of paper. "Make a couple of spares just in case I need to send out some more later on."

"Good idea."

While she waved her wand over the paper, I signed each duplicate as she handed them to me and then sorted them into piles according to the region or town that I needed to send them to.

"You have five minutes until your meeting with the council," Carmilla said from over my shoulder.

"Noted." So much for getting to take a nap beforehand.

I'd barely slept the night before, both from nerves and from the fact that Carmilla had decided to sleep in my room to "guard" the sceptre and kept meowing in her sleep.

Tansy scampered across my shoulders and wrapped her fluffy tail around the back of my neck. "It'll get easier. I doubt they'll have you writing letters every day."

"Don't give them ideas," I murmured. "I think I'd rather have another magical duel with Aunt Shannon."

She hadn't offered her congratulations to me, but I preferred to put off the moment when I inevitably had to speak to her for the first time since her failed attempt to snag the Head Witch title.

"That's because you're better at practical magic than paperwork," she said. "There's nothing wrong with that."

"It's not exactly a huge part of being Head Witch." While the person chosen was generally a strong witch, that didn't mean they often got to *use* the sceptre's magic —another reason Grandma's warnings about assassins made me sceptical.

Besides, powerful magic did not equal expertise. I might have inherited my family's unique talent for speaking to and understanding any animal, but when I lost my temper, I had a tendency to lose my grip on controlling my magic altogether. Granted, it had come in handy when I'd had to chase off reporters and stop Grandma's killer from getting away, but not so much when it came to sitting in meetings.

Outside, a clicking noise from the office door next to mine indicated that Mum had left for the meeting. As the new leader of the Wildwood Coven, it was technically her first day on the job, too, though I doubted she felt as unprepared as I did. Before I could join her, she pushed open my office door without knocking, appearing in the entryway with her ginger-and-white cat familiar, Horace.

"Are you ready for the meeting?" Mum asked. "You'll have to leave your familiar behind. Chloe can keep an eye on her, or you can send her outside instead."

Tansy scampered onto my desk. "I don't mind staying in here."

"We might be a while." I turned to Mum. "What is the meeting about, exactly?"

"You'll be introducing yourself to the rest of the council, primarily," she said. "It's—ah, not typical for us to have a Head Witch who isn't up to date on current events, so we'll give you a rundown of the main ones."

"Thanks." *I think.* I hadn't exactly come to my childhood home expecting to end up tied to my old coven, much less to be put in charge of important decisions. Since the entirety of the past week had been dominated by arrangements for Grandma's funeral and the votes for the new coven leader and Head Witch, nobody had even begun to talk about the aftermath until now. Nobody had left me a list of instructions either, though if they had, I wouldn't have been able to find it amid all the paperwork in Grandma's office.

As I followed Mum and Horace out the door, Chloe cleared her throat behind me. "Ah, Head Witch? Is there anything you want me to do during the meeting?"

"Yes." I turned back to the office. "Chloe, can you arrange those papers from my desk in order of importance and pick out anything that needs to be urgently attended to when I get back?"

"No," Grandma interjected. "I don't want anything moved."

"This isn't your office anymore, remember?" Closing the door on her, I found Mum giving me a look I couldn't decipher. "I can't have her under my feet all the time. Besides, it doesn't give much of a good impression if everyone knows what's going on except for me."

"I hired Chloe myself," said Mum. "I'm glad to see you're making use of her."

Reading between the lines, she'd probably arranged for Chloe to work as her assistant when she'd assumed she'd be taking the title of Head Witch as well as coven leader. We both had a lot of adjusting to do, that was for sure.

"I hope Grandma lets her do her job, then." I hadn't a hope of sorting through all that paperwork myself. There was a good reason I'd opted out of working for the coven as soon as I'd been old enough to find an alternative, aside from the fact that I'd struggled to maintain a passing grade in most of my classes at the academy. Too bad the sceptre had seen to it that I didn't have a choice after all.

I followed Mum across the lobby to the meeting room, worry fluttering inside my chest. Aunt Shannon would be present at the meeting as a fellow council member, and I hadn't spoken to her since she'd been hauled out of my office after trying to steal the sceptre for herself. I wouldn't forgive or forget what she'd done anytime soon, including bullying my cousin Rowan so badly that she'd seen betraying the coven as her only way out.

I hoped Rowan was having a better day than I was. She'd moved out of my aunt's house yesterday at the price of giving up her membership in the Wildwood Coven altogether, and while Aunt Shannon had doubtlessly been furious, she hadn't been able to stop her.

Mum opened the door to a room containing a long table set with chairs. Everyone inside the room rose to their feet, which made me squirm with discomfort, but two members were notably absent at the moment, namely Aunt Shannon and my cousin Vanessa.

When Mum and I reached the table, she edged me towards the seat at the head and whispered, "You have to start the meeting."

I did? Nerves swarmed me as I looked at the faces watching me around the table. "We'll start by introducing ourselves. I am Robin Wildwood, Head Witch."

The title still didn't feel like it applied to me, but saying it aloud broke the tension among the others.

Mum spoke next. "I am Lady Wildwood."

I'd forgotten she'd be going by a new title now. This would take some getting used to. The others I mostly knew, though the council members from the Wildwood Coven weren't the only ones I'd need to get to know, since the town's other smaller covens had their own representatives and so did the ones in the neighbouring magical communities.

When the introductions were over, Mum said, "The Head Witch usually begins by explaining her actions, decisions, and achievements since the last meeting. Or since this morning, in your case."

What did they expect me to have achieved in an hour, really? Everyone looked at me expectantly, so I said, "I sent out responses to the congratulatory letters from the other Head Witches."

"And?" Mum pressed.

I fidgeted in my seat. "Each letter required a handwritten personalised response, so I haven't had time to get anything else done."

Mum's brows shot up. "That's not customary. A printed one would be fine."

"It was Grandma's idea." I should have known not everyone would have agreed with her, even her daughter.

One of the other council members raised her brows. "Is the former Head Witch offering you her counsel, then?"

More like nagging me from beyond the grave. "Yes, she is, as well as my new assistant."

"Good," said Mum. "You've entered the position at a busy time, so I thought it wise for you to have Chloe around to help you."

"I thought we were still in the mourning period," I said. "For Grandma, I mean."

"You'll work it out between yourselves, I'm sure," said Mum. "The funeral delayed some other events, so the familiar contest was moved to this week. The contenders will start arriving this afternoon."

A heartbeat passed before her words sank in. "The *what* will start arriving?"

2

Back in my office, I took a seat at my desk again and tried not to groan at the mountain of fresh paperwork which had materialised in the hour I'd been absent. At least Chloe had arranged the papers in order of importance, but I didn't have the time to check them all if I was expected to judge the preliminary round of a contest that afternoon. Wildwood Heath often hosted the sort of weird contests common to small magical communities, but I'd hoped I'd get some lead-up time to prepare before jumping into the deep end.

"What even is this familiar contest?" I asked Tansy, who came scurrying in after having spent a productive hour chasing birds around the garden while I was in the meeting room. "Do you know?"

"I don't know any more than you do," she said, hopping onto the desk. "Carmilla?"

Grandma's familiar lay napping on the windowsill and didn't stir, while the woman herself was notably absent.

"Grandma?" I called out.

"Don't bother her," Carmilla said without opening her eyes. "She had a very tiring day."

"She's a ghost." Unlike me, Grandma didn't require sleep. Not that I'd be getting a nap this afternoon either by the looks of things. I wouldn't be at my best if I was constantly sleep-deprived, but even magic couldn't make extra hours in the day materialise out of nothing. "Where's the information on this familiar contest, then?"

"Over there on the left of the desk." Chloe popped up from behind me and made me jump a foot in the air. I hadn't even known she was still in the room. "Sorry, I was tidying."

Tansy scampered over and handed me the topmost file from the teetering stack. "The event starts after lunchtime at the town hall."

"It's an athletic-themed contest intended for witches and wizards who have a strong bond with their familiars," I read. "Ah… Mum's organising this one."

"Yes, she's spent the last few weeks making preparations," Chloe said. "She had to take some time off last week due to the funeral, of course, but everything is set to go according to plan."

Good, because I didn't know the first thing about organising contests, and Mum hadn't clued me in until now. Given how she'd frequently rearranged my room when I was a kid or signed me up for social activities behind my back, I suspected that getting her to kick the habit of not telling me anything would be challenging even as Head Witch.

Tansy bounced across the desk in excitement. "I'm good at athletic challenges. Do you qualify to enter?"

"Probably not," I said. "I'm a judge and announcer,

which would make it a conflict of interest. I think the rest of the council would object."

Though I had to wonder if certain members would show up for the contest that afternoon, given that they'd skipped out on the meeting. Aunt Shannon had recently suffered a dramatic defeat in her quest to become Head Witch, so I was willing to bet she'd be looking to restore her reputation by any means possible. Winning a contest would certainly qualify.

I began to read through the file, but I didn't get very far before the door opened and Ramsey walked in—without knocking. His familiar, Prickles the hedgehog, sat on his shoulder.

"Robin," he said. "Good, you have the file on the familiar contest. Will you be ready to greet the contenders this afternoon?"

"I'm doing great, thanks for asking." Honestly. My brother had been nice enough to buy me the camera Mum had promised me in exchange for helping out in the Head Witch ceremony over the weekend, but I should have guessed he'd be back to his annoying self by now. "What do you mean by greeting the contenders?"

"A number of the contenders will be coming from outside Wildwood Heath, as it's a regional contest," he said. "It's customary for the Head Witch to greet the new arrivals in person as they fly in."

"I thought I was supposed to greet the entrants from this town too," I said. "I can't spend half the afternoon standing on a hillside and running the risk of being ambushed by reporters. I have work to do."

"Grandma—"

I raised a hand the way Mum did when she wanted

silence, and to my surprise, it worked. "If Grandma was capable of being in multiple places at once, then I'm not. I'll send my assistant."

"Chloe?" His gaze went over to her. "Isn't she supposed to be protecting you?"

Of course he knew about her, since he and Mum had doubtless put their heads together to discuss how to ensure I didn't embarrass the family. Grandma herself remained hidden from sight, but that was probably for the best, considering that being a ghost had in no way dissuaded her from trying to exert her own control-freak tendencies over me.

Wait... did he say protecting me? Was he concerned about assassins too? That was all I needed. "Protecting me from what, exactly?"

"Need I spell it out?" he said. "You are a target."

"It'd be nice if you could give me a list of all these people who want me dead," I said. "Grandma hasn't been very specific."

He dropped his voice. "Nobody would suggest such a thing openly, but there are rumours. The Henbanes talked to the press about how they don't expect you to last the month."

"I make a point of not reading that nonsense, Ramsey," I said testily. "Don't you have work to be getting on with?"

He looked down his nose at me. "Think about it, please."

"Way ahead of you." I had the sceptre at my side, and my reflexes were good. Better than my handwriting, anyway. "See you later."

While he departed, I turned back to the file on the familiar contest. Mum had certainly been thorough in her preparations, and I'd have my work cut out if I was expected to do exactly the same for any future events I was put in charge of. With Grandma no longer hovering over my shoulder, I risked getting out her laptop and clearing a space on the desk. "Chloe, do you know where Grandma wrote down her passwords?"

"I don't know," Chloe said. "I think your mother said she memorised them."

"She did *what*?" Of all the things to *not* write down. "She isn't here. Does Carmilla know?"

"Let me try." Chloe held out her hands for the laptop, and I gave it to her resignedly. "I'll see if I can figure them out."

In the meantime, I picked up the planner Chloe had left on the desk and checked the dates and times of the various meetings and events which would take place over the next few weeks. Then I went back to the familiar contest file.

"The contest will be spread over the next two days," I read. "Today will be the preliminary round to see who qualifies, and the bulk of the contest will take place tomorrow, with a trophy ceremony in the evening. Why is the event on a weekday and not a weekend? Do you know?"

"I believe it was postponed due to the funeral last week," Chloe said. "I can't get any of the most obvious passwords to work. I might have to reboot the laptop and start from scratch."

"You can do that?"

She gave a nervous glance in Carmilla's direction. "I'd need the Head Witch's permission first..."

"Meaning mine, not Grandma's," I surmised. "All right,

go ahead. If she objects… well, it's not like she can use a computer as a ghost."

I was probably speaking too soon, but the sooner I adapted this office for the digital age, the better. Leaving Chloe in charge of the computer, I returned to my files. As was typical when I got absorbed in a task, I lost track of time. At least until Grandma's voice rang out across the office. "What are you *doing* to my computer?"

"It's mine now," I told her. "And we couldn't get into it without your passwords."

"How dare you!"

Chloe sprang upright. "I'm sorry, Head… er, Mrs Wildwood. The Head Witch asked me to—"

"Put that down right now," Grandma commanded.

"Did you even use the laptop yourself?" I asked. "It looks like it's been gathering dust for years."

"The disrespect!" An angry breeze rose and knocked several papers off the desk. It also woke up Carmilla, who hissed in my general direction.

"Carmilla, can you please tell your witch that I need to use the laptop for work?"

"I don't mind you *using* it," said Grandma. "But she's *destroying* it."

"You vanished, and we didn't have the passwords," I said. "Besides, I'll need my own accounts."

"She will." Chloe ducked her head when Grandma glared at her. "I can access your emails if you give me the password."

"There's no time for that," said Grandma. "You have a contest to judge."

"It's that time already?" I checked the time, seeing that I had an hour left, but I'd need to grab some lunch on the way. "I have to meet the contenders at the town hall, right?"

"Exactly," said Carmilla. "If you're going to insist on snubbing the ones who flew so far from out of town to be here."

"Chloe," I said, ignoring Grandma's familiar. "Can you go to the woodland path and give the arriving contenders directions towards the right place for the contest? I'll wait at the town hall and greet everyone when they show up. That way nobody will be left out."

"Of course," she said. "Should I leave the laptop here?"

"Go ahead. Maybe Grandma will be generous enough to give me her passwords when we come back."

Grandma herself scoffed. "The sheer nerve. Don't you forget that sceptre!"

I nearly *had* forgotten to pick up the sceptre on my way out of the office. Ducking behind the desk, I lifted the long instrument into the air. At least it wasn't heavy, despite being a little too cumbersome not to draw attention. The glowing purple gem on the end was pretty noticeable too.

Tansy ran alongside me out of the office, while I did my best not to feel guilty for not being able to be in two places at once. Mum hadn't greeted the funeral's guests on the hillside herself, but then again, she'd been too busy trying to clean up the mess left behind in the wake of her mother's death as well as her suspicion that she'd been murdered. That was a better excuse than being overwhelmed like I was, but it was only my first day on the job, and I'd little expected to find myself playing my new role in front of a bunch of strangers.

Yet despite all the odds being against me, I'd been the

one who'd found Grandma's killer. If I'd managed that, I could judge a simple contest. Right?

Mum's office door was locked, so she must have already left for the town hall. I tried to lock up my own office, but Carmilla yowled at me from the other side of the door. "Don't you lock me in here."

"Are you sure you won't fall asleep again?" I left her to it, though, figuring that she might do worse than hack up hair balls on my desk if I locked her in. "This wasn't in the job description."

"No, it wasn't," Tansy said, running underneath my hand. "Ow. Watch where you're swinging that sceptre."

I adjusted my grip on the long instrument. "I don't know how else I'm supposed to carry it."

"Get a sheath or strap it to your back." Tansy flicked her tail in demonstration. "Wear it like one of the warriors in *The Lord of the Rings*."

"How do you think Grandma would like that?" I stifled a laugh at the mental image of her face if I showed up with the ceremonial sceptre sheathed like a medieval sword, though I had to admit it was a tempting idea. Even so, there wasn't an inconspicuous way to carry a giant stick the length of my arm, and I felt a dozen invisible stares on my back as I walked down the street from the witches' headquarters.

At least I could appreciate the sensation of the cool breeze on my face after a day indoors and the humming magic of the Wildwood which surrounded the whole town and which strengthened my family's magical powers. Even in the busy main street which ran through the centre of town, I could feel the connection to nature that I'd missed when I'd lived away from home. That alone was worth putting up with being Head Witch for. *I think.*

The farther I walked, the more heads turned in my direction. Not a new feeling for me, by any means, but it felt like an age since I'd last walked down the street. It'd been a couple of days since then, but my life had been completely upended in the interim. I held the sceptre in a firm grip and did my best to ignore the stares.

The enticing smell from Were's My Coffee? drew me to the doorstep of the cosy café, where I peered through the window to make sure there were no reporters inside. I'd chased off Clarice and Speck from the *Blue Moon* the previous weekend, but even the Head Witch couldn't ban the press from the entire town. When I was sure the coast was clear, I pushed open the door.

A sharp sensation in my ankle made me look down. Prickles the hedgehog stood between me and the way into the café, an expression of disapproval etched on his face. "What are you doing?"

"Buying coffee," I said. "And lunch."

"Didn't Chloe warn you about not buying food and drink which hasn't been tested for poison?"

"The werewolves aren't going to poison me." I couldn't believe even my brother's familiar had got in on the paranoia. "If I don't get some caffeine in me, the contenders won't see me at my best, I can assure you of that."

It wasn't as if the café's staff had known I was coming, and the shifters who worked there wouldn't dare risk the backlash of poisoning the Head Witch even if they'd been inclined to do so. Which they weren't. My brother and his familiar desperately needed another hobby.

"Go on, hop it," said Tansy. "*I'm* her familiar. I can protect her if necessary."

I stepped over the hedgehog and entered the café, hoping I might see my cousin Rowan inside. She'd used the money she'd inherited from Grandma to pay the deposit on her new flat, but she'd need to find employment soon. Maybe the café would hire her, but I'd sworn not to bring the coven's drama to her doorstep until the sting of her mother's treatment of her had worn off a little.

I also gave the tables a quick scan for Harvey Walton, the professional Sky Hopper player who I'd had a crush on at school and who had also asked me out on a date a few days ago. I didn't know when I'd have the chance to take him up on that offer, and he knew I was busy this week anyway, but it would be nice to have something to look forward to. Since Harvey wasn't anywhere to be seen, I left the café and took my latte and sandwich with me to the town hall.

Inside, I found a carpeted hallway with a desk and a couple of chairs positioned in front of the door. At the far end stood a pair of polished oak doors which presumably led into the hall itself, while several smaller doors on either side were marked with signs in Mum's neat handwriting. One room was designated as a cloakroom for the contenders to leave their wands in—all magical items were banned from the contest to prevent cheating—and the room next door was for the contenders to gather in before the contest officially began. A quick glance through the small window told me it contained enough chairs to seat at least fifty people, though only sixteen contenders would make the final cut to take part in tomorrow's main event.

"There you are, Robin." Mum walked out of the main hall, the twin oak doors swinging shut behind her. "You'll sit there in front of the door to greet all the guests. There's a list, so you can check their names are on there. We don't want anyone sneaking in who isn't supposed to be there."

"Ooh, what's in there?" Tansy scampered past Mum's feet to peer through the gap in the oak doors behind her.

Mum barred the way. "The hall is off-limits until the qualifying round starts. I've been working on this since the weekend."

"Exciting." Tansy hopped over to the desk, which had been set up near the front door, while I took a seat to wait for the contenders to show up.

I didn't have to wait for long. I'd barely finished my coffee when the first person showed up, who happened to be none other than my cousin Vanessa. Her sparrow familiar, Hector, perched on her shoulder. Interesting that she'd shown up for the contest while she and her mother had been mysteriously absent from the morning's council meeting. No doubt she'd have some excuse brewed up if I confronted her, so I put on the most pleasant voice I could manage when I addressed her. "Are you here for the contest?"

Vanessa gave me a blistering look. "What do you think?"

"Please leave your wand in there." I pointed to the room behind me on the left. "Then take your familiar into the waiting room. The hall is off-limits."

She didn't move. "You aren't entering with that squirrel of yours?"

"I'm a judge, so no." I kept my tone light and pleasant despite Tansy's tail furiously wagging from her spot on the desk. "Best of luck."

"A judge." Her words dripped with disdain, but I simply smiled and added her name to the top of the blank page listing all the contenders. If I had to guess, she'd wanted to trounce me in public, and I'd ruined her day by not entering. At the thought, my own mood improved considerably.

Vanessa slunk away into the waiting room while the other contenders began to show up with their familiars. Some were local, some not, but the next person I recognised was a dark-haired witch around my age with a few grass stains on her jeans and a blackbird perched on her shoulder.

"Piper," I said, relieved to see a friendly face. "You're entering?"

"Thought I might as well." Her familiar cheeped in response. "I know your brother's watching out for trouble, but I figured it wouldn't hurt to have a friend among the contenders."

"Definitely, since Vanessa's taking part in the contest."

Her nose wrinkled. "What's *she* doing here?"

"I think she assumed I'd be competing, and she couldn't resist the chance to show me up."

"Pity you can't enter," she said. "Tansy is great."

"Yes, I am," said Tansy. "I think I should at least be allowed to help with the judging."

"I don't see why not," said Piper. "You look tired, Robin."

"Thanks."

"I mean it," she said. "I work for your mum, remember? Not that pruning roses is anything like being Head Witch, but I know how hardcore your family is."

"She let you have the afternoon off, though?"

"Yes, she seemed keen to let me come and enter the contest," she said. "Maybe she wanted me to keep an eye on you. I figured you needed a friend here anyway."

"I appreciate it." Unlike my family, she wouldn't judge me for struggling with my new position. Besides, Piper had actually been present in town for previous contests, so she'd know how things worked. She gave a running commentary on all the contenders who showed up, while I did my best to remember who'd come from where and which familiars they had.

"Who won the last time?" I asked her.

"Someone called Roxy Denton," she said. "She has a raven familiar."

I'd seen at least four ravens on the way in, not to mention countless blackbirds and crows. In fact, the waiting room was now so crowded that I wondered if we should have asked everyone to wait outside instead. It didn't help that the animals took up twice as much space as the humans and made a lot more noise, as I found when I opened the door to check on the contenders.

A scuffle from one side of the room drew everyone's attention as two wizards squared up to one another while a stripy cat yowled from a nearby chair.

I stood on tiptoe, holding up my sceptre in case I needed to use it. "What's going on?"

"His cat tried to *eat* my rat familiar," said a wizard with greasy dark hair, which looked like it hadn't been washed for a while.

"He was only playing," protested the other wizard, a slightly better-groomed individual with curly red hair who seemed to be the owner of the stripy cat.

"Oh, like when he and that other cat were throwing him around like a toy?" said the greasy-haired wizard.

"Don't you dare drag my familiar into it!" an annoyed voice rang out from among the others.

"That's enough." I raised the sceptre higher, which unleashed a bolt of bright purple light into the air. I hadn't intended to do so, but everyone in the room fell silent. "No more fighting. Save your energy for the contest."

I returned to the entryway, where Chloe had reached the front desk and picked up the clipboard. "I think that's it for the contenders. You'll need to go in and welcome them."

At least I knew how to get their attention. "Okay. Can you hang onto the clipboard?"

At that moment, the door slammed open, and a pale, mousy-haired woman carrying a chicken in her arms sprinted into the town hall.

"Sorry," she gasped out. "I took a wrong turn on my broom. Am I too late?"

"No, but I think you're the last." I indicated the clipboard in Chloe's hand. "Sign up there."

She gave her name—Anne Rafe—and then hurried to join the others in the waiting room. I waited a moment longer to make sure there weren't any more latecomers before following her inside. From there, I made my way to the front of the room by stepping around familiars and their owners, having to hold the sceptre at an awkward angle to avoid accidentally poking anyone with it. People mostly gave me a wide berth, though, and I reached the front of the room without tripping over anyone.

I faced the crowd and cleared my throat. "Welcome to the Familiar Contest. To those of you who are new to town, welcome to Wildwood Heath. I'm Robin Wildwood, the new Head Witch, and I'll also be helping to judge the contest."

"And I'm Tansy," said my familiar, scampering up to join me. "I'll be helping judge and keeping an eye out for cheating."

A murmur went through the crowd. If some of their familiars were likely to try to *eat* the others, then cheating might be the least of what I had to deal with. Good job I had Piper and Chloe helping me out.

"This afternoon's trial is intended to eliminate those of you who aren't ready to qualify for the contest," I told them. "You'll compete until sixteen of you remain for tomorrow's contest. The rest of you are welcome to stay in town for the duration, whether you compete or not. Meanwhile, there is to be no use of any magical objects, and everyone who meets the qualifications for the final sixteen must agree to leave their wands in our custody until the contest is over." That one was Mum's idea, though I suspected it was more to prevent the contenders from hexing one another than from using spells on themselves.

A discontented mutter travelled among the contenders, but nobody challenged me. The sceptre's presence helped, but as long as I stuck with the established rules from the previous contests, they shouldn't have any complaints.

"The preliminary round will begin shortly." I looked to Chloe for confirmation.

"This way," Chloe said, beckoning to the contenders to follow her out of the waiting room and through the oak doors into the main hall.

I could see why Mum had refused to let Tansy into the hall earlier, because the large space had been completely taken over by what appeared to be several obstacle courses, consisting of ladders and bridges and slopes. They varied by size, but they were clearly designed for familiars rather than humans.

Mum addressed the contenders from the front of the hall as they filed in. "You'll be divided into groups according to your familiar's species before being assigned an obstacle course challenge. The first four from each group to complete the challenge will advance to tomorrow's contest. Everyone else will be disqualified."

Chloe took charge of dividing up the contenders into groups according to their familiars' species. The cats and birds formed the largest groups, and the others ranged from frogs to goats and even the chicken—which caused a lot of confusion, because its owner claimed her chicken wasn't a good enough flier to compete fairly against the other birds.

I could see why this round had been designed as a process of elimination because of the sheer number of people who couldn't follow basic instructions, let alone their familiars, half of whom seemed disinterested in the obstacle courses. Instead, cats lay down to take naps, birds flew up to perch on the high ceiling, and other animals got into fights with one another. Chloe rushed around, breaking up these scuffles, but it wasn't my job to do anything but watch and judge the victors.

Among the bird familiars and their owners, Roxy Denton—a tall lean witch with straight dark hair—reached first place with her raven, and Piper won second place, but Vanessa scraped in third and would be advancing to the next round too. Among the cats, the stripy cat from earlier came out as the victor, to the evident pleasure of his owner. Lastly, there were the miscellaneous familiars, among whom the greasy-haired wizard's rat narrowly won out over the late arrival's chicken.

I had to employ the sceptre's glowing effect to quiet down the grumbling of the losers when the race came to an end. "There'll be plenty of other contests, don't worry. The preliminary round is over."

"All of the winners are to follow me, please,' Chloe said.

The sixteen qualifying contenders followed her out of the hall and back into the waiting room, while the others remained in groups next to the obstacle courses. At a gesture from Mum, I made to follow them, only for a loud screech to come from the waiting room.

As I entered, the chicken familiar ran in frantic circles around the waiting room, screeching, "She's dead, she's dead!"

The mousy-haired witch lay sprawled on the floor, unmoving, while her familiar shrieked and flapped her wings. "Dead!"

3

The chicken's shrieking stirred the other familiars to start making noise too. Even with only fifteen of them in the waiting room and not dozens, they created such a cacophony that Mum closed the door behind them, presumably so the noise wouldn't disturb the other contenders waiting in the hall.

Unfortunately, that meant trapping us all in the same room as the body of a woman who'd been perfectly all right not a minute beforehand.

"What happened to her?" My gaze travelled over the other fifteen contenders, all of whom looked confused or shocked. "Who saw?"

"She just… fell over," Piper said, appearing as stunned as the others. "Out of nowhere."

Mum's sharp gaze travelled among them while her familiar, Horace, hissed at the stripy cat when he wandered too close to the witch's body. "Every one of you is to wait in this room while I have the body removed."

I assumed she'd included me in that number, so I stepped aside as she raised her wand and levitated Anne Rafe's body out of the room. The chicken ran after Mum, still squawking, while I faced the remaining finalists and caught Vanessa giving me a derisive look. A prickle of doubt travelled down my spine. Had she somehow arranged for someone to drop dead in order to make me look like a failure of a Head Witch? Surely even she wouldn't go that far. I'd believed her and her mother guilty of murder before, and I'd turned out to be mistaken, but the timing seemed suspicious to say the least.

Piper took a step towards me, worry etched on her face. "Is there anything you need me to do?"

"Can you keep an eye on the others and make sure nobody tries to sneak out?" I whispered. "I should probably be with my mum while she figures out the cause of death."

"Of course," she said. "I'll let you know if I hear anything suspicious."

I trusted that she'd keep a close watch on Vanessa in particular, so I followed the sound of the chicken's screeching and found that Mum had levitated Anne's body into an empty room.

"She's dead!" wailed the chicken.

Mum gave me an exasperated look. "Can't you calm that bird down?"

"Calm down." I crouched next to the chicken. "Did you see what happened to Anne? How did she die?"

Even with magic, making someone drop dead out of nowhere wasn't exactly something one ran into every day.

I cast my mind around and found two possible explanations: poison and a deadly curse, neither of which was easy to pull off in public.

The chicken collapsed into a sobbing heap of feathers. Tansy scurried into the room behind me and gave her a thwack on the head with her tail. "Behave."

The chicken continued to sob, so I got to my feet and joined Mum beside the table where she'd placed Anne's body. "How did she die? Do you know?"

"If I had to guess, a maleficent curse." She pursed her lips. "Such a curse can only be placed upon an object, not a person."

"An object?" My mouth went dry. "Like what?"

"That is what I intend to find out," she said. "Do call your brother, won't you?"

"Right. I will." I pulled out my phone, my thoughts swirling in circles, and called Ramsey's number. "Come to the town hall. We have a problem."

Mum arched a brow when I ended the call. "You aren't going to tell him what it is?"

"He's literally a minute away. I bet he already heard the noise." I trod closer to Anne's body despite my instincts urging me to step away. "Is she holding anything?"

Anne's hands were folded across her chest, making it difficult to see, but Mum stepped in my way. "Don't touch the body. Leave the examination to your brother."

"If there's a cursed object in here, we need to know."

She hadn't dropped anything, and most curses were single use only, but a curse was a seriously nasty way to kill someone. Vindictive. And definitely a witch or wizard's work. Not that I'd suspected otherwise.

"Your brother will find out," Mum said. "He has the expertise. It should also be easy for him to find out which contenders have a personal connection with her."

"Right, because otherwise, they're all suspects." Why would any of them have had her killed, though? She'd placed second in her category, but the only gripe the others had had with her was for refusing to enter her chicken in the bird category. Hardly an offence worthy of murder. "A curse seems a bit extreme for a familiar contest."

"Don't underestimate what some individuals are willing to do to win."

"Like Vanessa," I muttered. "A curse seems a bit too sophisticated for her, though."

She'd also thought she would be competing against me, but that might have been Grandma's paranoia talking. All the same, what if Anne hadn't been the intended target? If Vanessa wanted me dead, there were more direct ways to go about it... but perhaps that was precisely what she'd wanted me to think.

Their paranoia is definitely rubbing off on you.

The chicken howled from the corner, and Tansy shook her head at her. "I know your witch is dead, but if you want us to find who killed her, you're going to have to cooperate with us."

The chicken merely howled in response while I could hear a similar level of noise coming from the waiting room. I hoped Piper wasn't having too much trouble keeping everyone from kicking up a fuss about being shut in there instead of celebrating making it into the contest, but I'd left Chloe in charge of the disqualified contenders in the hall, and she couldn't be in two places at once any more than I could.

As I'd hoped, Ramsey showed up within a minute with Prickles perched on his shoulder. "What's going on?"

"There you are." Mum beckoned him into the room. "Anne here was killed by a curse of some kind."

"She's dead?" he asked. "How?"

After "how," I heard the unspoken question directed at me: *How do you always get into these situations?*

I wish I knew, was the honest answer. If someone was trying to upend my first week as Head Witch, they'd certainly succeeded, but it was equally likely that someone was desperate enough to win the contest to eliminate the competition by any means possible. Everything had happened far too fast for me to know for sure.

"A curse," Mum said. "Placed on an object, I believe. I checked, and she didn't drop anything."

"Let me see." Ramsey walked over to her body at the table and pulled his wand out of his pocket. A flick caused Anne's clenched hand to open, revealing a ballpoint pen. He then gave the pen another complex wave, and a wisp of greenish smoke stirred from the end of the pen. "Yes… that's where the curse came from."

"*That's* what the curse was put on?" The pen looked utterly mundane, but when Ramsey checked her other hand, he found nothing else.

"Oi," Tansy said to the chicken. "Did you see how she got that pen?"

Ramsey jumped when Anne's familiar let out another shriek. "She—pulled it out of her coat pocket!"

"She didn't leave it in the other room." She'd arrived late, but the other contenders had been told to hand over any magical objects in their possession when they came in. Either she hadn't done so herself, or she hadn't realised it was there.

"Where are the other contenders?" asked Ramsey.

"The fifteen other finalists are in the room over there." I pointed to the door opposite. "The others are in the main hall. Chloe is watching them."

"I'll give Chloe instructions to search the disqualified entrants for any hidden magical objects," Mum said. "Is the curse defunct?"

Ramsey waved his wand over the pen then picked it up between two fingers. "Yes. It won't harm anyone who touches it."

My stomach turned over. "Did someone slip it into her pocket?"

"They wouldn't have been able to touch it with their bare hands if they did," Ramsey said. "Not without falling victim to the curse themselves. That's the risk with those types of curses."

Mum made to leave the room, saying over her shoulder, "I can trust you to take control of the questioning?"

"Of course," said Ramsey. "Who exactly am I talking to?"

"The other finalists, I assume." I pointed to the opposite room. "They were near her when she died. Not that that proves anything."

On the other hand, Vanessa was among them, and she sat firmly at the top of my suspect list at the moment.

"I'll call the rest of my team in to examine the body," he said. "Curses aren't my area of expertise, but I'm not sure we *have* a curse expert on the team. As for you..."

"As Head Witch, shouldn't I be present for the questioning too?" I glanced at Tansy for backup, and she scurried over to my side.

"Should she?" Ramsey, traitor that he was, looked at my mother instead of me.

"It's up to her," Mum said, to my surprise. "Go on, get on with it."

I might have been relieved that she'd given me the chance to get involved, but the grim expression on her face reminded me of when she'd suspected Grandma was murdered. Did she suspect I might have been the intended target myself? Or was she giving me another chance to prove my worth as Head Witch? I'd have to ask later, but Vanessa was in the next room. Her mother had been willing to go to almost any length to wield the sceptre, and her daughter had backed her up at every step. I doubted she'd had the sudden desire to win a trophy in a familiar contest, and competing directly against me wasn't the only means she had of undermining my authority as Head Witch.

"Did you leave the other finalists unsupervised?" he asked.

"Piper is watching them," I said. "Don't look at me like that. Chloe's busy with the ones in the hall, and I had to help Mum and deal with that chicken."

The chicken in question gave another despairing screech. "She's dead!"

"This one is being a great help," said Tansy. "Pity, because she might be able to tell us something useful about how her witch died."

"You watch her, then." Ramsey made to leave the room.

"Me?" Tansy said. "What about *your* familiar?"

Ramsey turned his head. "What about him?"

Prickles stuck his head over Ramsey's shoulder. "I'm helping Ramsey question the suspects."

Tansy made a rude noise. "You aren't doing anything. Come and help me talk some sense into this ridiculous chicken. Maybe threaten to sit on her if she doesn't quieten down."

"And someone needs to watch Anne's body while Mum is out," I added. "Until the rest of the team shows up. You can be nice to the chicken, can't you, Prickles?"

The hedgehog climbed off Ramsey's shoulder, wearing a long-suffering expression that matched his owner's. "Fine."

While our familiars stayed behind, I accompanied Ramsey into the neighbouring room to join the other fifteen finalists. After closing the door behind him, Ramsey's gaze went straight to Vanessa. Maybe he'd had the same thought as me. *See, I knew I wasn't just paranoid.*

Piper wore a relieved expression when she came to greet us. "Hey, Ramsey. Did you find out how Anne died?"

"I'm not at liberty to discuss the details with potential suspects," he said. "I intend to question each of you individually. Who would like to offer to speak to me first?"

Nobody volunteered, so Ramsey picked out a skinny blond wizard with a tuxedo cat familiar to come into the neighbouring room, which also happened to contain the wands and magical objects that had been given up by the contenders. I didn't see any pens among them, but I gave that side of the room a wide berth as Ramsey and I pulled out a desk and a couple of chairs at the front in which to conduct the questioning.

Ramsey had been through these scenarios before,

because he had a set of standard questions that he asked each contender, ranging from the person's background to which magical community they'd come from and who they knew among the other contenders.

"Did you know Anne Rafe before you came here?" he asked the blond wizard, who turned out to be called Patrick Wellman.

"No, she came from another town," he replied. "We'd never met before today."

"Did you speak to each other at all?"

"No," he said. "Though… she and that other witch got into a bit of an argument, I saw."

"Who?" I asked. "What other witch?"

"The one who looks a bit like you."

Vanessa. "What did they argue about?"

"How Anne refused to pit her familiar against the other birds," he said. "Something along those lines."

I turned to his cat familiar. "Is that true? Did you hear as well?"

Patrick blinked, looking as surprised as the tuxedo cat did. "You understand him?"

"Of course I do," I said. "My whole family can understand animals."

The cat dipped his head. "I didn't hear anything else, Head Witch."

When the pair of them left the room, I whispered to Ramsey, "We should question Vanessa next."

"We need proof before we can accuse anyone," he said in a low voice. "I have to question all fifteen of them anyway, just to be certain."

If I accused Vanessa, Aunt Shannon would be furious, but doing so without any proof was liable to end badly.

She might have lost out on the sceptre, but my aunt possessed enough cunning for several regular people.

Despite his obvious reservations, Ramsey called Vanessa in to be questioned next. My cousin entered the room with her sparrow familiar perched on her shoulder, a sour expression on her face.

"You're not with the police," she said to me.

"No, I'm not," I said. "However, I'm Head Witch, so I'm here to sit in on the questioning."

A muscle twitched in her jaw as she sat down. "Get on with it, then."

Ramsey didn't need to ask all the standard questions given that he knew her town and occupation perfectly well. Instead, he began by asking, "Is this your first time entering the contest?"

"No."

"You don't enter every year?" I asked.

She gave me a withering look. "Is this relevant?"

"Yes," said Ramsey, with a better poker face than I'd ever achieve. Admittedly, he didn't necessarily *enjoy* making her squirm. He was just doing his job. If she'd tried to wreck my first day on the job by murdering someone, though, then she deserved more than a little discomfort.

"No, I don't," she said. "Anything else?"

"I heard you had an argument with Anne Rafe before she died," I said. "About her chicken not qualifying as a miscellaneous familiar."

She tapped her manicured nails on the desk. "So what? A chicken is a bird. She was ridiculous to claim otherwise."

"I'm not saying you're wrong, only that she died right

after your argument."

Her eyes narrowed. "You want to kick me out of the contest, don't you? You're scared I might actually win."

"Hardly," I said. "I think we both know you don't care about the prize either way."

Ramsey shot me a warning look, but Vanessa spoke first. "Unlike some people, I follow through on my commitments."

Okay, that was underhanded. I might have turned my back on my coven several times in the past, but I'd made the conscious decision to do my best with the hand I'd been dealt despite wanting to do anything but take on the title of Head Witch.

Ramsey cleared his throat. "To return to the subject at hand, do you have anything else to say about your argument with Anne Rafe?"

"No," she said. "If she thought I was being mean to her, then it's her problem."

"Not now she's dead, it isn't," I said.

A flush spread across the bridge of her nose. "I didn't kill her. Unlike some people, I can keep my magic under control."

"It wasn't magic. It was a cursed pen." I ignored the jab at my magical prowess. "Expensive and rare. Can most contenders afford it?"

Her flush deepened. "You don't know anything about the others. You didn't even read the file, did you?"

"I did, despite spending my morning in a council meeting," I said. "Lady Wildwood was displeased when both you and your mother failed to show up."

"Was she now?" said Vanessa. "My mother and I had an urgent appointment with our lawyer, since you corrupted my sister into taking the money from our inheritance before she left our house."

What? "I thought she inherited the money for herself."

"No, we received it jointly," she said. "She took her share without telling me *or* our mother, so we had to check with the bank and with our grandmother's lawyer to make sure she hadn't taken more than her fair share."

"And she hadn't?"

"No, but she had some nerve going behind our backs like that."

More like no choice. Rowan had been backed into a corner, but I hadn't realised how thin a line she'd walked. If she hadn't left when she did, life in Aunt Shannon's house would have got even worse after her mother had lost her bid to become Head Witch. Rowan had already had her allowance cut off, so she'd been dependent upon working for the coven to earn a living and was consequently trapped under her mother's roof. The money Grandma had left her had been her only way out, and I refused to feel sorry for Vanessa or Aunt Shannon for the way she'd been forced to sneak around behind their backs.

"If you have a problem with what she did with Grandma's money, you're free to consult Grandma herself," I said.

"What?" she said. "She's not still here."

"Yes, she is," I said. "Her ghost never left, so feel free to pay her a visit. I'm sure she'll be thrilled."

I'd assumed she already knew about my incorporeal

office companion, as did Aunt Shannon. The upside to Grandma's presence was that Vanessa would have to think twice before breaking into my office for any reason, but I hadn't realised Grandma had kept herself hidden from everyone except me.

"Maybe I will," she said. "I'd like to hear what she thinks of how you're handling the job."

I refused to be goaded. "I'm sure she'll have words to say about you and your mother skipping the council meeting this morning."

A muscle twitched in her jaw. "My mother would appreciate it if you remembered who has done the most work for the coven over the last few years, because it's never been you."

"That's enough," Ramsey said. "We've heard all we want to know."

"Good." She got to her feet and left the room, the door slamming shut behind her.

I breathed in and out, aware of the fluttering in my fingertips as my magic reacted to my mood. "What do you think of that?"

Ramsey gave me a sideways look. "I think we ought to finish questioning the others before we jump to conclusions."

"It's hardly a big leap to make," I said. "Besides, she *did* skip out on this morning's meeting."

That didn't mean she'd spent the morning procuring a cursed pen, but for all we knew, she'd made up the story about visiting lawyers as an excuse. I'd need to ask Rowan for the details on how she'd gone about securing her inheritance. But either way, I'd royally ticked Vanessa off this time.

Did she really want to win the contest? I doubted it was a priority, but winning *and* humiliating me would be an appealing prospect. Still, the fact remained that I had no proof of her guilt. Not yet.

I'd see if any of the other contenders had anything more to add before I made a judgement call.

4

After Vanessa, the next contender to enter the room was Piper. Ramsey insisted on going through the standard list of questions, but they didn't faze her in the slightest. No surprise given that she'd mostly entered the contest to act as moral support for me, and she didn't expect to win.

"What did you say to Vanessa?" she asked. "She looked pretty mad."

"I reminded her that she skipped this morning's council meeting." When Ramsey gave me a sideways look, I ignored him. "Did you hear anything suspicious when you were with the others?"

"Depends what you mean by 'suspicious,'" she said. "Malcolm Harker's cat familiar keeps trying to chase the smaller animals, but that's all I saw. Oh, and there's a lot of noise coming from the hall. I think people are getting a bit restless."

"I guess some of them expected to be allowed to go home tonight if they didn't qualify," I said.

"They all have an offer of free overnight accommodation in one of the town's inns," Ramsey put in. "The offer is open to all the entrants, not just the ones who qualify for tomorrow's contest."

If everyone chose to stay, then that gave us barely more than twenty-four hours to catch the killer before all the entrants went home. "How far have most of them travelled?"

"Not that far," said Piper. "The contest only covers a handful of magical communities in the West Midlands, so there's no more than four or five towns represented here."

"So a lot of them might have come from the same place as Anne did," I said. "And the ones who didn't might have competed against her before."

"Exactly," said Piper. "Do you have any suspects yet?"

Ramsey frowned at her. "It's not appropriate for me to tell you the details, Piper."

"Ramsey, come on," I said. "You know Piper has no reason whatsoever to have cursed anyone."

"I can't even cast a simple nosebleed curse without it backfiring on me," she said. "As for the contest, I didn't expect to get into the top sixteen, to tell you the truth."

"Do you usually watch the contest?" I asked curiously. "Are there are any recurring entrants who might be rumoured to engage in suspicious behaviour?"

"I have the list of past contest entrants," Ramsey interjected. "I think that's all for now, Piper."

Honestly. As Head Witch, I was supposed to be unbiased, but Piper and I had known one another since we were kids, and I knew better than to factor her in as a potential murder suspect.

"Sure," she said. "Let me know if you have anyone you want me to keep an eye on."

"The usual." She'd know I meant Vanessa, so I waited for her to leave the room before shaking my head at my brother. "I don't suspect Piper, Ramsey. She's the least likely culprit, and she only entered the contest to keep an eye on the others for me."

"I know, but given the circumstances, it's better not to show bias."

"She isn't Rowan." It'd shaken me to learn that Rowan had told tales on the family to the press, I freely admitted, but I wouldn't get very far as Head Witch by shutting out my friends. "Where's the list of past winners, then?"

"I have it at my office," he said. "The list doesn't tell us which contenders knew one another personally, though."

"If their primary motive was winning, it doesn't necessarily matter." Not that I was moving Vanessa off the top of my suspect list, and her own motives would have had nothing to do with the contest.

The rest of the afternoon passed in a similar manner, with each entrant coming into the room one by one. The reigning champion and her raven familiar didn't seem bothered by the questioning, but then again, judging by her track record, she didn't need to worry about defending her title. She'd have no reason to kill off the competition.

When I mentioned this to Ramsey after she'd left the room, he said, "Maybe not, but she and Anne did come from the same town. In fact, all the top-ranked performers did."

"Do they have a gift like our family has?" Not that it was strictly necessary to compete in a contest. Maybe their town had a particularly stringent familiar-training programme at their academy instead, for instance.

"No, they don't," he said. "With that being said… the next contender is Persephone Henbane."

"Henbane." The name set off several sparks of suspicion in my mind like fireworks. "I didn't know any of *them* were entering. Is she related to Tiffany, then?"

"She's her niece." Ramsey called her into the room, and I studied the short thin witch who entered, wondering how I could have overlooked the resemblance earlier. She hadn't stood out among the other contenders, but she wore the bright clothing typical of the Henbanes and had a little black crow perched on her shoulder next to her cloud of dark-brown hair.

Ramsey wasted no time in jumping into the questioning. "Have you entered any contests before?"

She spoke in a high, tremulous voice. "I entered last year."

"And how did you perform?"

"I placed fourth." She hovered nervously on the edge of her seat. "I hoped to do better this time."

Placing fourth meant she'd narrowly missed out on a prize. That had to sting, especially for a Henbane witch. I'd bet Tiffany hadn't been pleased with her.

"Is the contest important to your coven?" I asked.

"Yes," she said. "Very."

I studied her, wondering if she might be as calculating as Tiffany under her nervous demeanour. Tiffany had tried to manipulate me into giving up part of my coven's property at my grandmother's funeral of all places, so she wasn't what I called a good role model.

Ramsey moved on to the next question. "Have you met Anne before?"

"I saw her at the last contest, but she didn't enter."

"Didn't she?" I looked at my brother in surprise, wondering if he'd known. He must have, given that he had the list of past entrants and winners.

"No, she was a spectator." She fidgeted. "I think she was there to cheer someone else on."

Interesting. I'd have to check with Anne's familiar, assuming we could get a single word of sense out of that chicken.

"Is there any particular reason you want to win?" I asked. "Did you enter for yourselves or on behalf of your coven?"

"A bit of both," she said after a moment's hesitation. "My familiar and I might not be able to understand one another's speech like that Vanessa and her familiar, but we're close, and I think we can win."

An interesting comment to make. My family were the only people I knew who *could* speak to and understand our familiars, and while I'd admittedly forgotten the contest entrants wouldn't have the same advantage, was her comment aimed solely at Vanessa or towards me as well? Tiffany's jealousy of the Wildwoods for being the leading coven in town was well-known, after all.

"That's all," said Ramsey. "You can leave."

Persephone rose to her feet and left while I watched her close the door behind her. "I should have remembered Vanessa would have an unfair advantage over the others."

"Not necessarily," said Ramsey. "Roxy Denton's raven familiar still beat hers in the qualifying round."

"Do you think Persephone is a likely suspect, then?" I asked.

"There's no direct proof, but given her history with our coven, it's safe to say she has a motive to disrupt the contest."

"Have you been talking to Grandma's ghost?" I asked. "Do *you* think I was the intended target? Because if I was, my would-be killer missed by a mile."

"That might not be the case next time." His expression was dead serious. "We can't rule out the chance that this is an attempted strike against the Head Witch."

"Are you sure it isn't just a petty rivalry? This seems too indirect a way to murder the Head Witch."

"So is poison."

I gave him an eye roll. "Speaking of which, I'd appreciate it if you didn't send your familiar to ambush me outside the coffee shop. I didn't become Head Witch to give up my lattes."

Ramsey made a noise that sounded like a repressed sigh of exasperation. "Prickles and I are simply concerned for your safety, Robin."

"I know." The camera he'd bought me over the weekend was proof that under his hedgehog-like exterior, my brother did care about me. I just wished he and Mum could let go of the image of me as someone they could mould into the perfect Head Witch and let me be my imperfect self for once. "Okay. Next contender."

Despite Persephone's presence here, I still ranked Vanessa at the top of my suspect list. Come to think of it, she'd even said she was here on behalf of her mother, which ought to be a red flag for Aunt Shannon's involvement. I mentally added my aunt to the suspect list alongside her daughter and waited for the next suspect to enter the room.

Next up was Malcolm Harker, the owner of the striped cat who had a liking for chasing other people's familiars. While that seemed dubious behaviour to me, Malcolm didn't give any answers which roused my or Ramsey's suspicions, so we let him leave.

The last of the fifteen entrants to be questioned was the young wizard with greasy black hair who owned the rat familiar that Malcolm's cat had tried to take a bite out of. The wizard, called Nolan, let his familiar walk at his feet rather than carrying him like the others and answered Ramsey's questions in a nervous voice.

"You came from the same town as Anne Rafe," Ramsey said. "Did you know one another?"

Nolan shook his head. "Not really."

"And you haven't entered a contest before?" I asked.

"No." He glanced down at the rat curled up underneath his chair. "I only acquired a familiar recently, so we weren't ready for the last contest."

Interesting, though not necessarily worthy of suspicion. My coven might have adopted the practise of getting young witches and wizards their own familiars as soon as they started classes at the magical academy, but not all towns had the same process as ours did.

"Did you speak to Anne at all?" Ramsey asked.

"Ah… she snapped at me when I suggested she should enter her chicken familiar against the other birds and not in the miscellaneous category," said Nolan. "She seemed a bit on edge."

"You weren't the only one who made that suggestion," I said. "Did she respond?"

"She told me to mind my own business." He fidgeted in his seat. "It's not really fair that her familiar could fly and ours couldn't, that's all."

"I'm guessing she didn't see things that way?" Ramsey asked.

"No, she seemed really tense," he said. "I wonder if she might have known something was wrong?"

I frowned. "You think she knew someone was going to curse her?"

He shook his head. "I don't think so, but what if that pen was already in her pocket? Nobody searched her on the way in, did they?"

No, they hadn't, but she'd arrived last of all the contenders, and I didn't recall her removing her coat. Unless she'd intended to give the cursed pen to someone else and had accidentally touched it first, but that didn't seem right either. Admittedly, lethal curses were more likely to backfire on their creators than not, so that kind of mishap wasn't unheard of. That was what made it such an unreliable way to assassinate anyone, especially a Head Witch.

Ramsey addressed Nolan's rat familiar with his next question. "Was Anne's chicken acting oddly during the preliminary contest?"

The rat stared at him for a second and made a shuffling motion which I assumed was meant to be a shrug.

"He doesn't talk?" I asked.

"Talk?" Nolan looked startled. "Wait, you can understand other people's familiars as well as your own?"

"Yes, all animals," I said. "Not just familiars."

He looked a little discomfited. "That must be... disruptive."

"You might say that," I said wryly. "Did he see anything?"

The rat shuffled back under the chair without speaking, but Nolan said, "No, neither of us did."

The questioning ended without any obvious red flags, but when Nolan reached to pick up his familiar and leave the room, he recoiled with a yelp, and the rat scurried away from his hands.

"Everything okay?" I asked.

"He bit me. Happens sometimes." Nolan let his familiar walk at his feet instead of picking him up, and I watched his tail disappear from sight through the door.

"Not well trained, is he?" I whispered to Ramsey. "Though I suppose they only recently became wizard and familiar."

"The rat isn't very talkative either," said Ramsey.

"Well, Malcom's familiar did try to eat him earlier," I said. "Do you think someone gave the pen to Anne before she arrived?"

"It's certainly a possibility," he said. "Nolan and Anne were both new to the contest, but there's not necessarily a link between them."

"We need to talk to that chicken to find out if she saw anything herself." She was the expert on her owner, too, but I could still hear the occasional distressed squawking noises from the other room. "What about the contenders who are in the hall? Are you going to talk to every single one of them?"

"The rest of my team will help," he said. "I don't think it's worth you staying to supervise the entire questioning, though."

"Probably not," I said, thinking of the small mountain

of paperwork awaiting me back at my office.

Before we could leave the room, Mum entered, wearing an irritated expression on her face. "Dealing with those contenders and their familiars is like herding cats. Literally in some cases."

Horace slipped into the room behind her. "I'll choose not to take that as an insult. Are we really offering free accommodation to every one of those contenders?"

"We have to if we don't want to risk the killer getting away," I pointed out. "How are they going to be organised? Will the finalists be staying in a different inn to the contenders who were knocked out in the preliminaries?"

"Not necessarily," Mum said. "I organised the bookings with the town's inns myself before the contenders arrived, and most of them intended to watch the contest tomorrow regardless of whether they got through or not."

"Better hope none of them is planning another attempted murder," I said. "How can you safeguard against that?"

"We'll be keeping all the potential contenders' wands locked in this room for the duration of the contest," Mum said. "Also, all of them have been searched for any magical objects, including cursed pens. We should have done a thorough search as they entered the town hall, but it's done now."

If that was an attempt to blame me for not being cautious enough, I didn't appreciate it in the slightest. "A cursed pen was not on my radar as a threat. Did you figure out whereabouts it came from? Because we'd rule out half the candidates on financial grounds alone if they had the funds to hire someone to put a lethal curse on a pen. If they did it themselves, it's not a common skill."

"Precisely," she said. "The curse was likely cast by an independent expert rather than the person who carried it."

"So they stood less of a chance of being tracked." There were ways to identify the source of a curse, though that was more my brother's team's area of expertise than mine. "We didn't ask the suspects about their skills at using curses. Would that show up in a background check?" Unless we dragged up all their grades from the academy, I imagined not.

"Did you not find out anything of note from your questioning?" Mum asked Ramsey.

"I can give you a report," he said. "Robin is going back to the office."

"Is she now?" I might have made a dig about technically having the authority to give *him* orders, but Mum ignored my tone.

"Good," she said. "You can take that chicken back with you."

"Excuse me?" She had to be joking. "I won't be able to get any paperwork done with a chicken screaming in my ear." Especially with Carmilla and Grandma's ghost already hanging out in my office.

"You can figure out how to deal with her, I'm sure," she said. "Go and fetch your familiar."

Tansy. I was betting she wasn't thrilled at having been left to watch the chicken for the past couple of hours, especially in the company of Prickles as well. I left Mum and Ramsey to talk and headed to rescue her.

Tansy ran over to meet me at the door as soon as I walked in. "I thought you'd forgotten about me."

"Sorry I left you in here." I let her scurry up my arm

and sit on my shoulder. "Mum insists that I have to take the chicken with me."

"Good." Prickles the hedgehog sat on top of a table near where Anne's body had been, while the chicken was still sobbing in the corner. "She's been absolutely impossible since the police removed the body."

"It's not fair," the chicken wailed.

"Calm down." I crouched next to her. "I'm going to take you out of here, but I'd appreciate it if you stopped screaming."

"Where are you taking me?" She howled when I tried to pick her up while Prickles gave me an exasperated look, as if it was somehow my fault that I couldn't calm down a traumatised chicken.

"Use a sleeping command," Tansy hissed in my ear. "I think it's the only way to get her home without her destroying our eardrums."

"Right, of course." I didn't like using that sort of magic on other people's familiars, but it was that or listen to her screeching all the way home. I leaned forward and whispered a command to her, and the chicken dozed off mid-yell, her eyes sliding closed.

I gingerly picked her up with one hand while awkwardly gripping the sceptre in the other.

"She'll be furious when she wakes up," said Prickles.

"If you have a list of other ways to quieten down a hysterical chicken, then feel free to ask Ramsey to send them my way." I walked out of the room with Tansy perched on my shoulder. "I can't take her into the office. She'll have to go and live in the garden for a bit."

I was less than enthused at the notion of carrying her through the middle of town, especially as it proved incredibly tricky to keep my grip on the sceptre at the same time. I felt like I'd wandered out of a bizarre role-playing game as I made my way through to the entryway.

Chloe came out of the hall to meet me by the door. "Are you going back to your office?"

"Yep," I said. "Can you do me a huge favour and carry this chicken for me? My mother insists that she can't stay here, but I don't think Carmilla wants her in the office either."

"Right." She gave me a dubious look, but she took the chicken from my hands.

I adjusted my grip on the sceptre. "Thanks. I wouldn't be much of a Head Witch if I dropped my weapon."

"It's not supposed to be a weapon." Mum's voice drifted through the partly opened door. "It's a symbol."

Not enough for the person who wanted me dead. If I had indeed been the target, then the Head Witch was supposed to be able to protect herself. The sceptre was a wand, not an ornament.

The door to the contenders' room opened, and Piper walked out. "Thought I heard your voice. Are you heading back?"

"Yes, but I don't know if you're allowed to leave."

"I got the all clear from your brother." She and her familiar walked behind Chloe and me. "Your mother implied that she expects me to spend the evening catching up on trimming the roses in her garden."

"Generous of her," I said wryly, checking the time. "I should only have half an hour of the working day left, but I get the impression the Head Witch's working hours never actually stop."

"Nah, you can set your own hours," said Piper. "Most Head Witches do."

"Grandma is intent on me not breaking with tradition."

"She's not in charge," Piper said. "Seriously, you could move all your meetings to the middle of the night if you wanted to."

"Her ghost thinks she is," I said. "Besides, I doubt the council will be impressed if I request that we move all meetings to the afternoon so that I have the chance to properly wake up first."

She shrugged, a mischievous glint in her eyes. "The vampires do everything at night already."

"There's never been a vampire Head Witch, though." There'd been a wizard or two, but Ramsey had removed himself from the running when he'd become head of the local police force. He didn't mind living and breathing work, but being trapped in a small room all day was my idea of hell. My delivery job hadn't been perfect, but at least I'd got to travel and see new places rather than staring at the same four walls.

"Is she being really tough on you?" Piper lowered her voice. "Your grandmother, I mean?"

"Sometimes it's deserved, but the rest of the time, not so much." I shook my head. "She got mad when I wanted to use her laptop instead of writing everything on paper, for crying out loud. There's a difference between giving me pointers and insisting I do everything her way."

"You two need to have a talk," she commented.

"Or I can use the chicken to distract her." If I set her loose in the garden, she might end up being eaten by a fox, but I drew the line at letting her roam around my office.

On the other hand, if I kept the chicken under close watch, maybe she'd recall some details of her witch's death that she hadn't already told us.

As we passed Were's My Coffee?, I saw my cousin, Rowan, standing outside the café's door. Piper gave her a glare, not quick to forgive her for telling tales on my family to the press, but it felt like a lifetime since we'd last spoken, and I'd already decided to give her a second chance. Once she was out of her mother's suffocating presence, she wouldn't have to choose between her family and her freedom.

Did she know Vanessa might be scheming against me? It was worth asking, so I gave Piper a nod to indicate she could go ahead with Chloe and the chicken. Tansy jumped off my shoulder, watching my cousin warily as I approached her.

Rowan gave a hesitant smile. "I heard you've had a rough first day on the job."

"From whom?" The words came out a little more confrontational than I'd intended. Perhaps I wouldn't fully trust her again for a while after all.

"I saw your brother and his team walking past and heard a bit of their conversation," she said. "A witch was murdered at the contest, right?"

"Yes, and we assume one of the contenders was the culprit," I said. "Also, did you know Vanessa entered the contest?"

"No," she said. "It doesn't surprise me, though. She likes winning."

"She claimed to be competing on behalf of her mother."

Rowan grimaced. "I bet. My mum has Vanessa there as her eyes and ears, I imagine."

Maybe she was trying to avoid showing her face in public. "Weird choice of a contest, though. She and Hector aren't close to one another. Do you think she's likely to cheat in order to win?"

"If anyone can catch her in the act, it's you," she said. "As for whoever killed that other competitor… I don't know if they'd have gone to those lengths just for a trophy."

Perhaps not, but I wouldn't strike Vanessa off the top of the suspect list yet. "Regardless, your mother *and* sister both skipped this morning's council meeting."

"As a snub, I'd guess," she commented. "They're mad at you."

"According to Vanessa, you took the money from your joint inheritance without asking permission," I said. "Supposedly, it's my fault for corrupting you."

She snorted. "You didn't. Also, I took exactly half of that money. I don't care a bit what Vanessa does with her share."

Unless she's buying cursed pens. "You still have enough money to get by for a while, right?"

"Sure, but I'm trying to convince the café to hire me." She glanced over her shoulder. "I think it's going well so far."

"That's great," I said. "I hope they give you a job."

While she had Grandma's money for now, what she really needed was long-term certainty that she wouldn't ever have to depend upon her mother for security again. And to ensure nobody sabotaged her attempt to make a new life for herself.

"Same." Her eyes widened as she looked over my shoulder. "Hey, we have company."

I spun around and spotted none other than Harvey Walton approaching us. The handsome tall dark-haired man contrasted with my memories of him when we'd been students at the academy, though I'd had a huge crush on him even when we'd both been awkward teenagers. I'd never fallen into his orbit at the time, since he'd spent most of his free hours on a broomstick while I'd struggled through remedial lessons for classes I'd failed. The knowledge that he'd even remembered my name had floored me, to be honest, but I hadn't even begun to consider the feelings that had developed between us before I'd found myself shoved into the position of Head Witch and with zero time for a dating life.

Tansy scampered up my shoulder and nudged me. "Go on, talk to him."

Rowan grinned. "I'll see you soon, okay?"

At another nudge from Tansy, I closed the distance between Harvey and me. "Hey."

"Hey," Harvey said. "How're you getting on?"

Where to start? He might not know about Anne's death yet, and my brother would not be thrilled if I told him. "Things are… busy. I'm judging the familiar contest."

"Oh, I did wonder if you'd be taking part," he said. "The main part of the contest is tomorrow, right? So you're free tonight?"

He doesn't know. It was hardly the topic for a date, and I had a stack of paperwork waiting for me back at the office besides. "I have a bunch of stuff to do tonight, but I might be free later this week. After the contest is over."

"Robin Wildwood!" Carmilla stalked towards us, her

fur sticking up in all directions. "Your grandmother wants you back at the office."

Harvey gave her a dubious look. "You know that cat?"

My face went bright red. Of course he couldn't understand her, so her words presumably sounded like yowling to everyone in the café witnessing the Head Witch getting yelled at by a cat. Wonderful.

"Yes... she's Grandma's familiar," I said. "Hang on a second."

I hurried over to Carmilla, who sat on the street corner, her amber eyes reprimanding me. "Slacking off already?"

"Since when do you ever leave the office?" I hissed at her. "I'm not slacking off. I'm walking home."

"You're still on duty as Head Witch," said Carmilla.

"Not until I get back to the headquarters, I'm not."

"Wrong." She jabbed at my ankle with a claw. "You're always on duty, even when you're asleep."

I hopped out of reach of her claws and gave Harvey an apologetic look. "I'm sorry. I have to get back to the office."

"That's fine," he said. "Let me know when you're free, okay?"

"Sure." I scowled down at Carmilla. "Don't you have someone else to annoy? Like your owner?"

Carmilla simply yawned and then padded away. I couldn't believe my deceased grandmother's cat had stunted my dating life for the foreseeable future, but that was what I got for assuming I'd ever be allowed to have a moment's peace—even after a murder on my first day as Head Witch.

5

Fuming, I made my way back to the office and found Chloe sitting at the desk, brow furrowed as she used the laptop. Grandma's ghost floated into view when I walked in, and I shot her a scowl. "Thanks a bunch for sending your familiar to yell at me in public."

"You're welcome," she said. "Your assistant got back before you did, so I assumed you got distracted."

"I was talking to my cousin," I said. "Who also happens to be the sister of one of the suspects in today's murder."

Chloe looked up sharply. "You were talking to a suspect? Without me there?"

"Rowan isn't a suspect, but I thought she ought to know about her sister's involvement in the contest." I studied the laptop Chloe was using. "What are you doing, anyway?"

"Setting up your accounts."

I gave Grandma a look. "You don't have a problem with her using your computer?"

"Chloe respects my authority."

"You don't have any authority," said Tansy. "You're a ghost."

"You're proving my point," Grandma said. "Right, Carmilla?"

Her cat yawned. "She's also conveniently forgetting to mention that Rowan wasn't the only person Robin met with."

Thanks for that. "There's nothing in the rules of being Head Witch which prevents me from saying hi to a friend."

"A friend who seems *very* interested in whether you're free tonight," said Carmilla. "He's *that* one, isn't he? The one who's rumoured to be *great* at riding a broomstick."

"Is he now?" Grandma's ghostly expression turned intrigued at the suggestive note in Carmilla's voice. "Do you have personal experience, Robin?"

I groaned. "Go away, both of you. I have work to do."

I did my best to ignore her cackling in the background while Chloe picked up the computer and vacated the desk. Piper must have taken the chicken to the house with her, thankfully, because listening to Grandma and Carmilla make crude comments about Harvey was quite enough without adding a screaming chicken as well.

"Don't you have your own desk?" I asked Chloe, seeing that she'd set the laptop on top of a filing cabinet instead.

"No," she said. "Should I?"

"Yes." I looked at Grandma. "Did Stacy have her own desk?"

"Don't talk about *her*," she snapped. "She's the reason we're in this mess."

"By 'mess,' do you mean me being in charge?" Annoyance fluttered through me, and Tansy lifted her head as magic stirred to my fingertips. I clenched my hands in an effort to hide my temper. "Chloe, can you go to one of the classrooms and borrow a desk and chair until I can get you one of your own? I'm sure nobody will mind."

"Yes, they will," said Grandma.

I ignored her and gave Chloe a nod of encouragement. She left the laptop behind and ducked out of the room while I faced my grandmother's ghost. "Look, I'm aware that this office used to be yours, but my name is on the door. You don't have to like it, but I'd rather not be disparaged by my own family, especially as there are plenty of people who might be inclined to come up with a more permanent way to be rid of me."

"What do you think I was trying to tell you earlier?" She tutted. "Now someone is dead."

She couldn't seriously be blaming *me* for Anne's death. "If I was the intended target, then they missed me by a mile. You're welcome to help Ramsey with the investigation if you have a problem with the town's security. I'm sure he'd be thrilled to hear your input."

"There's no need to use that tone with me, Robin," she said. "As your familiar generously pointed out, I am a ghost. If someone is trying to curse you to death, then you have that sceptre for a reason."

"Mum seems to think it's an ornament." I placed the sceptre behind the desk as I sat down. "Also, I wasn't exactly on high alert for a cursed pen of all things. Did any assassins ever throw a cursed pen at *you*?"

"No," said Grandma. "Did I hear you've been talking to suspects?"

"I could hear you and Ramsey talking to them through the door," Tansy said. "I have theories."

"So do I," I said. "Vanessa is at the top of my list."

"I bet she did it," said Tansy. "Even if you weren't the target, she wanted to make you take the blame for her death."

"What I'd like to know is where she got hold of a cursed pen," I said. "I can't imagine many of the contenders would be able to afford to commission a deadly curse to use against me."

Vanessa had the money she'd inherited from Grandma herself, but Persephone Henbane was another contender who might consider me a rival.

"Never underestimate the lengths some would go to in order to undermine your authority," Grandma said.

"Making a stranger drop dead of an unknown curse seems a bit extreme," I said. "If they had the pen cursed by an expert, is there a way to track the person who cursed it?"

"Not if they covered their tracks." Grandma tutted when Chloe hauled a desk through the door into the office. "You have the tools to find the culprit. Use them."

"What does that mean?"

Instead of answering, Grandma's ghost vanished. *That's the opposite of helpful.*

———

Despite a late night of dealing with paperwork, I found myself at the office the following morning before the sun had fully risen, going through the list of past contest entrants which my brother had generously left outside my bedroom door.

Admittedly, the main reason I'd come to the office this early was to avoid a certain chicken, who'd spent most of the night roaming around the garden and screeching loudly at the other birds. I was pretty sure that Mum and Ramsey had slept terribly for the same reason, so I'd left the house before I had to deal with their bad tempers and took Tansy with me to the office.

"Anne didn't enter any contests before this one," Tansy said, perching on my shoulder to read the file. "She was one of the few newcomers who advanced to the next round."

"Yep." I stifled a yawn, making a mental note to stop by Were's My Coffee? on my way to the first proper round of the contest. "Also, Roxy has won every regional familiar contest for the last three years, as well as some national ones."

None of the other entrants had that kind of prestige. I continued to read through the file until Chloe showed up to work on Grandma's laptop again before dealing with a few admin tasks. The stack of paperwork had grown again overnight, but Mum interrupted my attempts to reorganise my desk by opening my office door and walking in. "There's a problem."

"What kind of problem?" I asked. "With the contest?"

"With Anne dead, we need another contender to take her place."

"Why?" Oh, right. There were supposed to be sixteen participants in the contest. "Can't we pick one from among the others?"

"Do you think that would go over well with anyone who isn't chosen?"

She had a point, but I couldn't think of any other ideas for finding someone at the last minute. "I can't take part myself, can I? And Piper is already in the running."

"Can you think of anyone else?"

"Rowan?" I didn't miss her irritated expression at my cousin's name. "I can't think of anyone else in town with a well-trained familiar who isn't already in the contest. If you have any better ideas, I'm all ears."

She pursed her lips. "If you're sure, then go and fetch your cousin. I'll escort the other contenders to the starting point for the next round, which will take place at the end of the woodland trail."

It'd have been nice if someone had told me that earlier. "You mean outside of the town? Up on the hill?"

"Of course." She left the office while Chloe closed the laptop and left it on the desk next to where Carmilla lay napping underneath the window.

"I'm glad we get to go outside," Tansy said. "As long as nobody tried to murder each other during the night, it should be fun."

"Don't even." We couldn't have kept an eye on them from dusk until dawn, but surely Mum would already know if any more murders had taken place in the night.

I waited for Chloe to leave the office before calling out to Carmilla, "Can I lock the office this time?"

The cat didn't wake up, and her owner didn't reappear, so I locked the door behind me before leaving the witches' headquarters. I nearly tripped over the chicken on the doorstep, who made a disgruntled squawking noise. "Watch where you're going."

"What are you doing here?" At least she'd stopped screaming, but if she had trouble flying, I had no idea how she'd got out of the garden.

"I'm coming with you, of course," said the chicken.

"No, you're not," said Tansy. "You kept everyone awake all night."

The chicken shuffled closer to me. "I can't stay behind. A magpie keeps trying to attack me."

"Myrtle." I should have guessed Aunt Shannon had set her familiar loose on our new guest. "Sorry, that was my aunt's familiar. She doesn't like me."

"Can I come, then?" The chicken made a soft noise like a sob. "I'm sure Anne would want me to watch the rest of the contest. For her."

I exhaled. "Fine, provided you don't distract the other familiars. Chloe, can you take her with you while I go to speak to Rowan?"

Chloe nodded. "Of course."

"Thanks." I doubted carrying a chicken around had been in her job description any more than it'd been in mine, but after yesterday's humiliation with Carmilla, I didn't need any more animal-related incidents at the coffee shop. Besides, I still had to carry the sceptre everywhere I went. "I'll be there before the contest starts."

Tansy ran alongside me as I made my way down the street towards the centre of town. I stopped outside the coffee shop to make sure no familiars were about to ambush me again. None did, but Rowan sat at a table in a corner, sipping a latte.

I ordered one for myself before approaching her. "Hey, Rowan."

"Robin." She looked up at the clock above the counter.

"Aren't you supposed to be at the first round of the contest?"

"I have a slight favour I need to ask you first."

A wary expression appeared on her face. "What is it?"

"You know one of the contest entrants died yesterday. We need someone to replace her, and we can't ask any of the other entrants in case they accuse us of being biased."

She frowned. "You want me to enter this contest?"

"It's a contest specifically for people who have a strong bond with their familiars," I said. "I know it's a big thing to ask, considering your sister is also taking part, but…"

"I'll do it," she said. "If I can make life difficult for Vanessa *and* help you out, then I'm game."

"I appreciate it." It was also another chance for her to show her support for me after her interview with the *Blue Moon* had shaken my trust in her. I just hoped Vanessa wouldn't make her regret her choice.

The werewolf running the café handed me my coffee. "Good luck, Head Witch."

"Thanks." I paid for my drink before leaving the café with Rowan. "The first round is supposed to take place right at the end of the woodland path, but my mum didn't tell me what it actually involves."

"That figures." She let her tarantula familiar, Ralph, climb out of her pocket as we walked, while Tansy scurried at my feet. "You look tired."

"A chicken kept me awake all night. Don't ask."

I told her anyway, though, and by the time we reached the woodland trail, she was up to speed on both the murder and my dubious start as Head Witch.

"I can't believe Grandma's giving orders from beyond the grave," she said.

"I shouldn't be surprised, but she's proving more of a challenge than my *living* family members." I spotted a large crowd gathering at the far end of the path. "Here we are."

I found Mum standing with her back to the trees, facing the contenders. Chloe and the chicken stood with the larger crowd that had gathered on the hillside to watch, but Mum beckoned me to her side in front of the other fifteen contenders. A frown appeared on her face when Rowan came to join them. Maybe she hadn't expected my cousin to say yes.

Vanessa, on the other hand, wore an expression of shock and anger, but I simply smiled at her when she glared at me. Rowan, meanwhile, put as much space as possible between herself and her sister, though Piper didn't look thrilled to see her either.

"Now we're all here," Mum said, "I will explain the rules. The primary aim of the first round of the Familiar Contest is a test of trust between you and your familiars. All the humans will be blindfolded for this round, and their familiars will guide them along the racetrack beneath their feet."

I looked at where she pointed, belatedly noticing the trail painted onto the grass and winding across the hillside. It seemed most of the eliminated contenders had elected to come and watch the next round, since they filled the area on the other side of the track.

"Also," she added, "no familiars will be permitted to talk during this round. I will know if they do."

I hid a smile, figuring that that rule was there to prevent Vanessa from having an unfair advantage. Still, I resolved to keep an extra close eye on her in case she tried to thwart Mum's instructions.

At Mum's command, the contenders lined up at the start of the racetrack with their familiars at their feet.

"That will do," Mum said. "Put your blindfolds on— properly, Vanessa—and secure them tightly."

Both Mum and I watched carefully for any cheating while our familiars kept a close eye on the animals. The track itself was pretty straightforward at first glance, but once everyone had their blindfolds on, Mum raised her wand and gave it a wave. The grass on the hillside changed, creating a swampy area at the foot of a steep slope while a tangle of bushes sprang up near the finish line. This was going to be tricky.

"I heard that, Vanessa," Tansy shouted from next to me. "No whispering to your familiar. That's cheating. If you do it again, you're disqualified."

Vanessa flushed, but her familiar flew off her shoulder and landed at her feet instead.

"Both humans *and* familiars are to wait behind the starting line," Mum ordered. "Robin?"

Oh, I was supposed to start the round. I held up the sceptre so that its glow was visible to the crowd watching in anticipation. "Begin."

The race started, the contenders moving forward. Some flat-out ran, some were more cautious, but they all ran into trouble almost at once as they sank up to their knees in the swamp. There was no shortcut available, and the familiars who couldn't fly were forced to climb onto their owners to keep from sinking. Nolan's rat was not a fan of that, squeaking angrily as his wizard waded through the mud.

Roxy and her raven were the first to find their way out of the swamp, but Persephone Henbane and her bird and Malcolm and his cat were close on her heels. Rowan did decently well, though Vanessa overtook her when they escaped the swamp. I was sure my eldest cousin wasn't strictly adhering to the rules—it was hard for me to make out whether she and her familiar were exchanging whispers in the general cacophony of animal noises combined with the crowd cheering on the contenders.

The next hitch came at the steep slope that followed the swamp, where several contenders tripped over or slid back down the hill due to their muddy shoes. Roxy and her raven remained in the lead, but half the contenders were still stuck in the swamp by the time she reached the top of the hill.

Things grew heated when Malcolm's cat yowled, a sharp and sudden noise that startled almost all the other familiars into leaping into the air or running in panicked circles. Roxy and her raven took a decisive lead, while Rowan actually gained ground because her familiar wasn't scared of sudden noises. Vanessa, meanwhile, ended up going in the wrong direction entirely until she skirted the edge of the woods.

Tansy snickered with laughter. "I hope she gets lost in the forest."

Fortunately for Vanessa, the other contenders had lost most of the ground they'd gained, and the few that had both escaped the swamp and scaled the hill found themselves stalling when they reached the thorny, tangled bushes near the end. The thick undergrowth brought even Roxy and her raven to a standstill while the crowd screamed encouragement.

Vanessa and Persephone had almost caught up to her when Roxy escaped the trees and reached the finish line. The crowd's screaming grew to a crescendo.

"The race isn't over until *eight* of you have crossed the finish line," said Mum. "Let go of that blindfold, Vanessa."

I glared at my cousin, not that she could see me. She was third to reach the finish line, behind Persephone Henbane, with Rowan in fourth. The rest took a while to catch up, and Nolan and his rat and Patrick and his cat were among the next four contenders to cross the finish line.

Half the rest were still stuck in the swamp when Mum called the race to an end.

"Remove your blindfolds, please." I had to raise my voice over the clamour from the audience while the noise had sent the chicken into a screaming fit again.

"Quiet," Mum said. "This round of the contest is over. Remember, if you reached the end of the race, then it doesn't matter who won. There are still three rounds to go."

Until then, the contestants had an hour to clean themselves up before the next round. Everyone was covered in mud, animals and humans alike, and it'd been harder to spot any cheating than I'd anticipated. Except for Vanessa, of course, and Malcolm's familiar's blatant attempt at distraction.

"Should I talk to him?" I asked Mum. "Malcolm, I mean? You heard his cat yell to distract the others on purpose."

"He didn't cheat, technically," she said. "And why did you bring that chicken?"

"Aunt Shannon's familiar has been harassing her," I

said. "I'll use another sleeping command if she keeps screaming."

"I thought I taught you not to use your magic on others' familiars."

The chicken's wailing cut through my attempt to reply. "I think this qualifies as an exception."

I had an hour to speak to the contenders, and I fully intended to do exactly that. Dealing with the chicken would have to wait until later.

6

After putting the chicken back to sleep and leaving her in Chloe's care, I followed the mud-covered contenders downhill along the woodland trail before singling out Malcolm and approaching him.

He gave me a questioning look when he saw me. "Something I can help you with, Head Witch?"

I thought I detected a hint of mockery in his tone, though I might have been mistaken.

"Why did your cat make that noise?" I asked. "Did you tell him to scare the other animals?"

"No," he said. "If they're scared of a little noise, though, they won't make it very far in the contest."

His cat meowed in agreement, walking alongside him downhill.

"Don't let it happen again," I said, but he didn't turn back.

"Hope he gets kicked out in the next round," Tansy whispered in my ear.

"Same." Out of the corner of my eye, I spotted Roxy and her raven walking nearby. As I watched, she murmured something to the raven, who replied with a low chittering noise.

When Roxy saw me, she slowed her pace. "Head Witch."

"Can you two understand one another?" I asked curiously.

"As well as any witch or wizard," she said. "Ah—except your family, that is."

"You have remarkable control," I said. "When Malcolm's familiar tried to startle everyone, yours is the only familiar who didn't react."

"That's right." She gave her raven a stroke. "We've been entering these contests for years. Nothing much fazes her anymore."

"I saw your record. It's very impressive." It was common for witches and their familiars to have an innate understanding that went beyond words, but they'd sounded more like me and Tansy talking to one another than a typical witch and her familiar. Still, that didn't mean either of them might be breaking the rules of the contest.

At that moment, someone else came into view who drove all thoughts of the other contenders from my mind. Aunt Shannon strode uphill, her blond curly hair flowing behind her in the breeze and her cloak swirling around her ankles. At the sight of her, tension zipped up my spine. After her absence from yesterday's meeting, I'd hoped that she'd sit out the entire contest and leave her daughter here in her place, though I knew better than to think she wasn't scheming with Vanessa behind the scenes. Maybe my inviting Rowan to take part in the contest had annoyed her enough to finally show her face.

"What do you want?" Tansy called out.

"How dare you." Aunt Shannon stopped in front of me, fury etched on her face. "The sheer nerve of you."

"You'll have to be a bit more specific." Frankly, I had no idea if she was referencing my new status as Head Witch or the fact that I'd helped Rowan go behind her back.

"As if it wasn't enough to betray your own family," she spat. "You schemed with the very person who conspired against her own *mother* in order to humiliate Vanessa."

Couldn't she even say Rowan's name? I'd been under no illusions that she'd be angry with me for my choice, but I'd—perhaps naively—assumed she'd be too busy licking her wounds over missing out on claiming the title of Head Witch to challenge me in public. As she glowered at me, the trees rustled around us with birds taking flight and animals stirring in the bushes in response to her rage. Adrenaline jolted through me, and I held the sceptre tight, prepared to use it if necessarily.

"I didn't recruit anyone." I kept my tone calm despite my own turbulent emotions. "I asked my cousin to enter the contest as a favour due to the death of another contender, nothing more. It wasn't an attempt to under-mine Vanessa."

"I suppose you'll make the same claim about how she took Vanessa's inheritance too."

"She took her fair share of the money Grandma gave her," I said. "Also, I had nothing to do with that. Take it up with Grandma if you have a problem with her giving money to Rowan—who, I might add, is an adult who's perfectly capable of making her own decisions."

"Maybe I will," she said. "She won't ever see another penny from me, I can assure you of that."

She'd disowned Rowan altogether? It didn't surprise me that she had, but I couldn't entirely rule out the possibility of her trying to ruin Rowan's new life in more indirect ways. "If you wanted her to stay in your house, then you shouldn't have cut off her allowance and forced her to work for the coven to begin with. You made her so miserable she had to find her own way out."

A dangerous glint appeared in her eyes. "Do you believe every word she tells you? She's a deceiver. Look at what she did to her own flesh and blood."

I had the sense I was facing a losing battle trying to convince her otherwise, so I changed tack. "Look, I wouldn't have asked her to take part in the contest if someone hadn't been murdered yesterday, leaving us one contender short. I needed a replacement who wasn't likely to cause trouble."

She gave a harsh laugh. "Both of you are nothing *but* trouble. You deserve one another."

"Thanks," I said as if she'd paid me a compliment. Which, in a way, she had. Rowan and I might have had our differences, but I'd sooner ride a kelpie without a saddle than do anything which might be comparable to the likes of Aunt Shannon. "Did you come all the way out here to yell at me? Or was there another reason?"

"Why would there be?" she queried.

"I thought you might have useful information to give me about the murder." I tried to read her expression, but her face remained inscrutable. "I'm sure you and Vanessa had time to discuss the subject at length."

"*I* am quite sure you can resolve this little problem yourself."

"It wasn't little. Someone died." Vanessa had entered the contest on her mother's behalf. Had Aunt Shannon asked her to do more than just secure victory? This wasn't the first time I'd suspected her of murdering her way to her goals, and I'd turned out to be mistaken, but that was before I'd snatched her dream straight from her grasp. "Can I help you with something else, then?"

"No." She looked me over. "No, I don't think you can."

"Mother!" Vanessa strode downhill and caught up to her mother, breathless. "That awful chicken bit me."

"What did you do to her?" Hadn't she been asleep and under Chloe's watch? If someone had woken her up, I'd place the blame squarely on the person with the ability to influence and communicate with animals who also had a good reason to cause a public scene.

"Why would you assume *I* did something wrong?" she said. "You're the one who was supposed to be watching that ghastly creature."

"No, Chloe is," I said. "Where is she?"

"I don't know, and frankly, I don't care," said Vanessa. "That chicken should be locked up. You shouldn't let it roam around."

"You're in a familiar contest," I pointed out. "If you hadn't wanted to be around animals, you should have entered the flower-arranging contest instead."

Tansy cackled at Vanessa, who scowled at me. "You put her up to this."

"If I could get that chicken to do what I asked, I'd have told her to stay at home," I pointed out. "Which is what I tried to do, except your mother's familiar kept terrorising her when she was in the garden, so I had to bring her here instead."

"*What* did you say?" Aunt Shannon gave me a glare to equal her daughter's. "You might be Head Witch, but that doesn't give you licence to disrespect me."

"So you're denying that Myrtle spent the night chasing the chicken around our garden?" It wasn't worth pressing the matter, so I turned my back on both of them. "Forget it."

Resigning myself to losing my chance to speak to the contenders, I retraced my steps uphill until I ran into Chloe, who was hurrying towards the forest.

"I'm sorry," she said. "Minty—she's gone."

"Minty? Who's that?"

"The chicken," she said. "I got her to tell me her name before the loud noise disturbed her. Anyway—a minute ago, she woke up and ran into the forest."

"Let me guess—Vanessa woke her up." I turned towards the densely packed trees of the Wildwood. "Sorry I left you alone with her. I should have known Vanessa would try something underhanded."

Tansy ran towards a tree. "I'll have a look for her. She can't have gone far."

"Unless she can fly better than she let on." I couldn't climb trees as well as Tansy, so I let her scurry up to the canopy to survey the surrounding forest. "Did you see which way she ran, Chloe?"

"That way." She pointed into the mass of trees. "Oh... I think there's someone in there."

"Is there?" I walked into the forest, skirting a large oak tree. That chicken was more trouble than she was worth. I should have known bringing her to watch the contest had been a mistake.

"Hey, Robin." Rowan popped out of the bushes, still covered in mud and grass from the race. "Is my mother still around? I ran in here as soon as I saw her."

"She's with Vanessa." I pointed vaguely towards the path. "Have you seen a chicken? Apparently, she bit Vanessa and then ran into the forest."

Rowan snorted. "I thought you put the chicken to sleep."

"I did, but Vanessa woke her up," I said. "You should go back home and clean up before the next round of the contest."

"I'd prefer to avoid my mother." She rubbed her grass-stained hands on her trousers. "Speaking of whom, I'm guessing she isn't happy I entered."

"No, but she blamed me for inviting you," I said. "Besides, won't it feel good if you end up winning against Vanessa?"

"Not if it causes her to try to ruin my new life." Rowan lowered her gaze. "I should probably drop out."

"No." She might have had a point, but dropping out of the contest wasn't going to make her mother any less likely to retaliate against her for turning her back on the coven and her family. "Don't forget I'm the one she's mad at. Besides, you know Vanessa doesn't stand a chance of winning the contest. That Roxy is pretty much a certain victor."

"Found her!" Tansy yelled from nearby.

Chloe, Rowan, and I moved through the trees until we saw Tansy's bright tail sticking out from a bush. Sure enough, a feathery lump sat underneath.

I crouched down at her side. "Minty?"

The chicken whimpered but didn't say a word or move.

"What did my sister do to her?" Rowan crouched next to me. "Ah… Minty… you shouldn't run off into the forest. You might get eaten by a fox."

"Not sure that's helpful, Rowan," I said out of the corner of my mouth. To Minty, I added, "I won't let Vanessa go near you again, okay? But we have to leave. Come with me."

Minty crept out from under the bush, and I kept an eye on her as we made our way downhill. We'd need to avoid the path if we didn't want to run into Aunt Shannon or Vanessa, but Minty jumped at every small noise in the bushes, and I had to stop her from running away again at least twice. Once we were far enough from Aunt Shannon to risk veering near the path again, I glimpsed Malcolm walking out of the forest himself, still covered in mud. At the sight of him, Minty gave another loud squawking noise and flapped her wings.

I shushed her, keeping an eye on Malcolm's back. "What's the problem?"

"Did you know him?" Tansy asked. "Malcolm, I mean?"

"Maybe his cat tried to eat her," said Rowan. "That was his cat causing trouble in the race, wasn't it?"

"Yes…" My frown deepened when I spotted someone else walking through the trees, too far away for me to make out their features. I squinted, seeing dark hair, a slight frame. "Is that Nolan?"

"What's he doing in here?" Rowan asked.

The chicken made a distressed noise and ran in

completely the wrong direction, forcing me to hurry to catch up to her. "Come back."

Minty ran in circles, flat-out refusing to set foot back onto the path, and I had to employ yet another sleeping command on her in order for Chloe to pick her up and carry her back to the woodland trail.

"You don't want her back in the garden, right?" Chloe asked. "There's a cage in your office, I think, so we can put her in there until she wakes up."

"What did Grandma need a cage for?" On second thought, I probably didn't want to know. "I'd let her roam around the coven's garden, but Myrtle might find her there too."

Keeping her sedated in the office wasn't exactly a great long-term solution, either, but I was out of any other ideas. Rowan and I parted ways at the end of the woodland path, while Chloe and I took the chicken to the witches' headquarters and found Carmilla sitting expectantly on the doorstep. "There you are. Where have you been?"

"I had to find a runaway chicken." I indicated the feathery lump in Chloe's hands. "What's going on?"

Carmilla stretched, arching her back. "Someone tried to break into your office."

Chloe nearly dropped the chicken. "What?"

My heart lurched. "When?"

"Less than five minutes ago," she said. "When you were gallivanting off."

"I wasn't gallivanting off." I'd been in the forest... and so, by the looks of things, had half the contenders. "Wait, did you see the intruder?"

"No, but I heard a male voice," said Carmilla. "I think he was casting an unlocking charm on the door."

"And?" I pressed. "What did you do?"

"The voice woke me up, so I yelled until he bolted."

"Where to?" I looked up and down the road, but the intruder would have disappeared by now.

"I'll look." Chloe set the chicken down on the doorstep and then hurried down the road, leaving me staring after her.

Who tried to break in? It couldn't have been Aunt Shannon unless she'd recruited someone else to do her dirty work while she'd been marching around the woods. Besides, my family was aware the office wasn't unguarded. On the other hand, the contenders might not have known it was under watch by a ghost and her familiar. Might one of them have tried to break in?

After picking up the chicken, I followed Carmilla into my office before examining the door as if in the hopes of finding signs of a mark from the intruder's wand. Chloe came running in a moment later. "I'm sorry, Head Witch. I can't find the intruder."

"They didn't get into the office. Don't worry," I said. "Grandma's ghost hasn't come back yet?"

"No." Carmilla hopped onto Chloe's desk. "Might I suggest leaving a mousetrap of sorts near the door?"

"I don't have a mousetrap." Or did I? If there was a cage somewhere among all those cabinets, then there might be a mousetrap too. "Carmilla?"

"Don't ask me." The cat yawned. "What is that chicken doing in here?"

"I need to find a cage for her," I said. "Or set her loose in the garden and hope Myrtle leaves her alone."

"I'll get the cage." Chloe ducked behind the cabinets, while I set the chicken down on the desk. Tansy, meanwhile, began opening the desk drawers and riffling through the contents.

"What are you doing?" I asked.

"Found it." Tansy hopped out of the drawer and held up an ink bottle. "This is invisible ink which glows in the dark. If you put that on the door, the intruder will be unmasked the instant you see them in the dark."

"I prefer the mousetrap idea, personally." Then again, knowing me, I'd forget and put my own hand in it. "All right."

I took the bottle of ink from Tansy and set about daubing it carefully onto the door handle. When I returned to my office, I found that Chloe had put Minty into a small cage.

"I don't think she should stay unwatched," she said.

"I know, but I can't carry her around everywhere either." I debated waking her up, but she'd raise hell when she found herself in a cage, and I didn't quite dare set her free in case she panicked and got herself lost in the woods again. "Put her out in the yard."

"Sure." She carried the cage out of the office, while I checked the time and found that I didn't have long before I needed to be at the contest's next round.

And to think I'd assumed that being Head Witch would mostly consist of attending tedious council meetings.

7

When I made my way back to the woodland path, Rowan called out from behind me. She'd changed out of her muddy clothes, but her boots were still caked in mud, and her blond hair was damp and windswept.

"Hey, Robin," she said. "Malcolm said the next round of the contest is a scavenger hunt in the forest. Not sure why he told me, but I'm not complaining."

"Huh. I didn't know." Was that why Malcolm and Nolan had been wandering around the woods earlier? "I didn't have time to ask, though, because someone tried to break into my office while I was gone."

"Your office?" She blinked in confusion. "Oh, you mean Grandma's old office. Who tried to break in?"

"No idea. Carmilla woke up when she heard someone trying to use a spell on the door, but she didn't see who it was." And Grandma's ghost had been inconveniently absent at the time. "It also can't have been Aunt Shannon or Vanessa, because I ran into them right before I got back."

She grimaced. "Yeah, that's weird. So the attempted break-in happened when we were looking for the chicken in the woods?"

"Yes." Which ruled out at least two or three of the contenders but not all of them. Persephone Henbane, for instance… though Carmilla had insisted the person she'd heard had been male. I'd definitely seen both Malcolm and Nolan in the forest, so who else did that leave? At least the ink I'd put on the door would clue me in if the intruder was foolish enough to try again, so there was nothing to do but try to put it out of my mind for now.

Rowan and I followed the woodland path, joining the other contenders heading in the same direction. Malcolm was among them, and I found myself wondering how he'd found out the nature of the second round of the contest when he'd seemingly spent the interlude wandering around the woods with his familiar. I didn't quite know what to make of him, to be honest. His familiar had been aggressive towards the other animals, but he'd also given Rowan information on the contest. Had he done the same for the other contenders?

I quickened my pace and caught up to Malcolm. "Hey. Can I have a word?"

"Another one?" He glanced down at his cat familiar, who flattened his ears at me.

"You knew this round was due to take place in the forest." No point in beating around the bush. "How'd you find out?"

"I heard someone telling… what's her name again? Vanessa?" he replied.

Aunt Shannon. Of course she'd wanted to give her daughter all the advantages she could get, and he must have overheard their conversation while he'd been wandering in the woods. Given that I'd seen Nolan in the forest, too, he might know as well.

"Is there any reason you told my cousin?"

"Which cousin?" he asked. "Rowan, right? I figured she'd want to know. It's only fair, since her sister already knew."

"Fair" was not a word I would have used to describe his behaviour so far, but unless he'd magically teleported himself back into the forest after breaking into my office, he couldn't be the intruder I was looking for. "I just wondered."

Tansy tugged on a strand of my hair. "Look who it is. I wonder what *he* was doing in the woods."

Nolan walked past, his rat scurrying along at his feet. I veered in his direction and caught him up. "Can I have a word?"

He gave a nervous nod. "Sure."

"I saw you in the woods earlier," I said. "Were you looking for the next round of the contest?"

"No, I got lost when I wandered off the path," he said. "I was looking for a shortcut back to the inn, but I didn't realise the woods were that twisty."

"You've never been to the Wildwood before?"

"It's not out of bounds, is it?" he asked. "I know it belongs to your coven..."

"No, it's fine." The only people officially not allowed in were reporters. "I take it you found your way back eventually?"

"Yeah, with two minutes to spare before I had to come

back." He gave an attempt at a smile. "That'll teach me to leave the path."

Hmm. He'd been wandering in completely the wrong direction, but I'd done the exact same thing on my first excursions into the Wildwood as a child.

A squeaking noise from by my feet made me aware that I'd almost trodden on his rat. "Oh, sorry."

The rat gave me a baleful look, but Nolan put on an apologetic expression. "Sorry. He doesn't like being held, so I have to let him walk."

"I thought not." His familiar seemed a little antisocial to say the least, and I was kind of surprised he'd lasted this long in the contest. Regardless, I knew he couldn't have been the one who'd tried to break into my office. Not unless he was capable of being in two places at once, that is.

The image of the chicken's freak-out when she'd seen him in the forest sprang to mind, but she'd already been panicking at the time, and I wasn't sure she'd even recognised him. Leaving her behind had been the best available option, I knew, yet I couldn't shake the feeling that I ought to have tried harder to get her to answer my questions about Anne's death.

In the meantime, I reached the end of the path, where the contenders gathered in the same spot as they had before the prior challenge. The winding racetrack had vanished, but the spectators' numbers had grown since the last round had ended.

Mum stood in front of the forest, Horace prowling around her feet, while Chloe talked to her in a hurried whisper. She must have been explaining the break-in and the chicken's absence. *Here we go.*

"Robin." Mum's gaze pinned me to the spot. "Why exactly didn't you inform me of the break-in yourself? Did you at least call your brother?"

"Carmilla said she scared off an intruder, but she didn't see who it was," I explained. "They never got into the office, and I figured Ramsey would want more proof than that."

"You thought wrong." Her eyes narrowed. "You also seem to have lost that chicken."

"She's in the coven's garden," I said. "She ran into the forest earlier when Vanessa decided to scare the living daylights out of her, so I thought it would be safer to leave her behind."

"I hope you made the right choice," she said. "As for the intruder, I'd advise you to take further measures to ensure that they won't escape next time."

"I will," I said. "Trust me, the next person who tries to break through the door will be easy to find."

"I looked everywhere around the building, but they'd already gone by the time we got there." Chloe wrung her hands. "I'm sorry, Head Witch."

"It's not your fault," I said. "They clearly ran fast, and it's not as if anyone actually saw them. Carmilla said she heard a masculine voice, but that covers a lot of people."

"We'll deal with that later." Mum's gaze travelled across the contenders on the hillside. "Everyone's here. Let's begin the next round."

Mum walked out to address the contenders, some of whom were still covered in mud from the previous round. Eight remained, and this round would bring that number down to four.

"For the second round of the contest," she said, "you'll

be divided into two teams. All witches and wizards will wait here on the hillside while your familiars hunt for a number of tokens in the forest and bring them back to you. The first team to retrieve ten tokens will win."

"So our familiars are going to do all the work?" Vanessa asked.

"No," said Mum. "Each of the two groups will receive a single map of the area, and you'll give your familiars instructions on how to find the tokens' locations. It will be a team effort, because all four members of the winning team will advance to the next round. The losing team will be disqualified."

A murmur of unease passed among the gathering contenders while the audience waited with bated breath. Everyone knew that if one team was weighted in favour of past winners, they were almost certain to come out on top.

To make it fair, Mum had written the name of each contender on a scrap of paper, which she proceeded to draw from a bucket, like a low-budget Goblet of Fire, or so Tansy whispered in my ear. I stifled a laugh, though I found myself as tense as everyone else when Mum began to draw the names for each team. Roxy and her raven both looked calm, but everyone else was visibly on edge, even Piper and Rowan, who weren't necessarily looking to go ahead to the next round despite the appealing notion of beating Vanessa publicly. Their familiars paced anxiously, and all eyes were on Mum when she drew the first set of names.

In the first team, Roxy and her raven were to compete alongside Persephone Henbane; Patrick, the skinny blond wizard with a tuxedo cat familiar; and Vanessa, who looked very smug when she saw Roxy was on her team. Persephone looked incredibly relieved, too, though she avoided my gaze when I looked in her direction.

Piper, on the other hand, found herself teamed with Rowan, Malcolm and his striped cat, and Nolan and his rat.

"The first team is to stand over there." Mum pointed to a spot partway down the hill's right side. Then she pointed to the left. "And the second team will wait there. You have five minutes to discuss strategy among yourselves before sending your familiars into the woods."

She handed each team a map of the forest which displayed the area the scavenger hunt would take place in. Good thinking, because while Piper, Rowan, and Vanessa were familiar with the Wildwood, the majority of the contenders weren't, and Vanessa wasn't exactly a team player. Typical that she'd ended up on the team of the reigning champion, but the attempted break-in had reminded me that the outcome of the contest was the least of my worries at the moment.

I watched both teams as they discussed their strategies for finding the tokens and winning the scavenger hunt. The second group was mostly silent, with Piper and Rowan studiously ignoring one another, and Malcolm and Nolan weren't particularly talkative, either. I caught Piper's eye and smiled before approaching the other team instead. The first group was a little more talkative than the other, with the exception of Vanessa. Maybe she hoped to coast through on Roxy's expertise, a plan which might actually work for her. The fact that she and her familiar knew the forest well would work in her favour too. While Roxy did most of the talking, Persephone and her bird were hanging onto her every word, with Patrick occasionally chipping in. Figuring I wasn't going to hear much of interest, I returned to wait with Tansy, Mum, and Chloe.

"I think we know who's going to win," Tansy whispered in my ear. "Shame, really. I'd have liked to see Vanessa knocked out by her sister."

"You never know." The contest had thrown in several surprises so far, and at least Vanessa staying in the contest meant she'd remain where I could see her. While she couldn't have been the one to break into my office, I wouldn't rule out her mother's involvement entirely. "Where's Aunt Shannon?"

"Must have taken off," said Tansy. "So much for supporting her favourite daughter."

"Your five minutes are up," Mum called out. "Head Witch?"

I raised the sceptre. "Begin."

Both groups of familiars departed for the woods while their owners looked on from their positions on the hillside.

Tansy bounced up and down on my shoulder. "Anyone in particular you want me to watch?"

Between Vanessa's antics and Malcolm and Nolan's wandering around the woods during the interlude, I had no shortage of potential troublemakers to keep an eye on, but after my chat with Aunt Shannon, my cousin still ranked at the top of the list. "Vanessa's familiar."

"Gotcha."

Tansy scaled a tree to watch from above as the familiars disappeared amid the forest. The two birds on the first team had an advantage over the familiars who had to walk on the ground, but Malcolm's familiar did his best to make up for it. I watched the tiger-striped cat climbing the trees and leaping between the branches with ease, though Roxy's raven easily outpaced him. Nevertheless, Malcolm's cat was the first to return with one of the painted tokens in his mouth, followed shortly by Roxy's raven. They remained more or less neck and neck, but smaller familiars like Nolan's rat were at a disadvantage compared to the larger or airborne ones. As for Rowan's tarantula, he remained nowhere to be seen until long after the others had returned at least one token each.

When Ralph finally emerged from the trees, he was limping, two of his legs bent at odd angles. Rowan called his name and ran to his side. "Ralph, who did that to you?"

I didn't hear Ralph's response, but Rowan gingerly picked up the tarantula and then glared at the other contenders. "Which of your familiars attacked mine?"

Nobody answered, but when Piper's blackbird was the next familiar to emerge from the forest, Rowan marched over to her. "Was it you?"

"What?" Piper held out a hand, and her familiar flew over to land on her. "Don't be ridiculous. We're on the same team."

"You don't even want to win, though, do you?" Rowan's face reddened. "I don't believe this."

"We have ten tokens!" Vanessa shouted.

Cheers rose up from among the other team, while Vanessa in particular looked incredibly pleased with herself. So did Persephone, though she backed away when she saw Rowan barrelling towards their team.

"Hey!" Rowan shouted at her sister. "Did your familiar attack mine?"

"Of course not," Vanessa said, and her blackbird chirped in agreement. "She was nowhere near that spider of yours. Maybe a wild bird mistook him for a snack."

"That's not funny." Rowan looked down at her familiar, who'd curled up in her hand. "You haven't heard the end of this."

Rowan stormed away to the woodland path. I found Piper standing beside me, wearing an expression of disbelief. "I don't believe she accused me of attacking her familiar."

"She's upset," I said in a low voice. "I think it was Vanessa. It must have been."

"It wasn't." Tansy scurried uphill to join me. "You aren't going to like this, but I was watching that sparrow the whole time, and he didn't go near Ralph."

"Then who was it?"

"Malcolm's familiar," she said. "I saw him take a few swipes at the others too."

"They were on the same team, though." That made no sense. Why would he attack his own teammates? "Is that cat of his really that badly trained?"

"I'd ask him, but he's gone," said Tansy.

I spun on my heel to face the other contenders, but both Malcolm and his cat were nowhere to be seen. "Where did he go?"

"I bet he ran off before he got caught," Piper said. "I knew there was something I didn't like about that guy."

"Really?" I asked. "Why?"

"He seemed... sketchy," she said. "He told me this round was going to be a scavenger hunt like he was doing me a huge favour."

"He did the same to Rowan. Said he overheard Aunt

Shannon telling Vanessa." His familiar's behaviour had rubbed me up the wrong way from the start, but I'd been so fixated on Vanessa that I hadn't thought to give him any more attention.

Mum raised her voice to address both teams. "You all have an hour until the next round of the contest begins. I'd advise you to grab something to eat and calm down."

The crowd began to disperse, winners and losers alike. Before Nolan could leave, I waylaid him. "Did you see where Malcolm went?"

"That way." He pointed downhill. "He looked like he was in a hurry. What happened?"

"It sounds like his familiar attacked Rowan's tarantula," I said. "Do you know why he'd turn on his own teammate?"

"No." He looked down at his rat familiar, who shrank backwards. "I guess he's not well trained."

"He attacked your rat yesterday, didn't he?" Not just him, either. "I have to find him."

Well trained or not, Malcolm and his cat had a track record in entering similar contests, so his behaviour couldn't be accidental. I ran to Mum's side, Tansy clinging to my shoulder. "What's the policy if one person's familiar attacks another?"

"Disqualification," she said promptly.

"Malcolm was already on the losing team," I said. "But attacking his own teammate makes no sense unless he was trying to lose on purpose."

"Robin, if you want to talk to him, by all means, do so."

"I would if I could find him." I turned away and rejoined Piper. "Malcolm is staying at the same inn as the others, right?"

"I assume he is," she said. "Do you think he's going to try to do a runner?"

"He might. I need to catch him first." I wanted to check that Rowan's familiar was okay, but her tarantula was pretty resilient after a lifetime of running away from her sister's and mother's familiars, and it was Malcolm I needed to catch before he and his familiar left town altogether. "Let's find out what he's up to."

8

Piper and I headed downhill, Tansy scurrying at my side. Malcolm didn't appear, which seemed to back up my suspicion that he'd gone straight back to the inn to prepare to flee town.

"Does he have a habit of doing this sort of thing?" I asked Piper. "His record says he's placed in the top eight in every contest he's entered but never higher."

"You're asking the wrong person," said Piper. "This is my first time entering the contest, remember? I know the names of the past entrants, but I couldn't tell you if any of them got up to anything dodgy."

"I know," I said. "Why would he sabotage his own team, though? I can understand him cheating to try to win, but this is different."

The murmur of voices behind me made me glance over my shoulder, and I spotted Roxy talking to Vanessa of all people. My cousin shot me a smirk when she saw me looking at her.

Keeping my expression pleasant, I approached the pair of them. "Did either of you see where Malcolm went?"

"Why's that?" Vanessa asked. "You want to ask him for tips on training that squirrel of yours?"

"No, I'd like to know why his familiar attacked your sister's," I said. "Considering they were on the same team."

I turned my attention to Roxy instead, but she simply looked confused. "Why would he do that?"

"Exactly what I'd like to know."

"Sounds like an excuse to me," said Vanessa. "It's typical of my sister not to accept defeat without a fuss."

"She didn't care about the contest," I told her. "She signed up as a favour to me. Not that you'd know anything about that."

I rejoined Piper, annoyance flaring inside me. It'd make far more sense for Vanessa to be responsible than Malcolm, but I had no proof of foul play on her end. I just had to hope she got thoroughly trounced in the next round.

Piper and I left the woodland path and continued down the main street into the middle of town.

"Which inn is Malcolm staying at?" Wildwood Heath had two main inns, neither of which was particularly big, so the contenders had been placed in hostel-type dormitories unless they'd paid extra for a single room. Roxy and her raven headed towards the Owl's Nest, the nearest inn, so Piper and I followed her. "Excuse me. Is Malcolm staying in here?"

"He is," she said. "I can see if he's in the dorm if you like."

"Thanks," I said. "I don't see him sticking around town

for long, not if he knows we're aware of what his familiar did."

"Nor me," said Piper. "He ought to be put on a banned list for future contests."

"Mum didn't seem too fussed." I belatedly remembered I'd left Chloe back with the other contenders, but at least I had Piper with me for moral support. "I know he's already disqualified, but still."

Roxy emerged from the inn. "Malcolm isn't here. According to the guy at reception, he hasn't come back yet."

"Weird." Was he still wandering around in the forest? He'd left all his possessions behind, including his wand, so he couldn't have sneaked out of town already, surely. "Right… I should grab lunch and head back to the office."

"Good call," said Piper. "I'll come and watch the next round of the contest if you like. Keep an eye out for trouble."

"Thanks," I said. "I expect Vanessa will get more and more desperate to win as we get closer to the final round."

"Yes, she will," said Tansy. "Also, you should go and check if anyone else has tried to break into your office."

"Good point." I'd have thought the intruder would've had more sense after their previous failure, but I was frankly lost as to why they'd break into the office to begin with. If they wanted me dead, there were stealthier ways to go about it than to risk drawing the attention of the entire coven.

Come to think of it, if Malcolm turned out to be the person who'd killed Anne, he didn't need to stay in the contest in order to reach another target. Being out of the spotlight might play in his favour. At the thought, I quick-

ened my pace when I drew closer to the coven's headquarters while Tansy hurried alongside me. She then
came to a dead stop, her tail sticking straight up in the air.
A sense of foreboding washed over me when I spotted
Chloe standing frozen in the doorway of the witches'
headquarters, her back to me.

"Chloe?" I asked. "What's going on in there?"

She swayed a little. "Oh… he's dead."

I approached the door, my heart plummeting downward. Malcolm lay on the lobby floor, one hand
outstretched and his eyes partially open. He was dead, all
right, and when I walked closer, I glimpsed what appeared
to be a pen in his outstretched hand.

Chloe moved to let me past, her expression stunned,
while I mechanically reached for my office door handle.
Locked. He hadn't got inside. No… someone else had
reached him first.

How is that possible? If he was the pen's owner, then it
made no sense for him to have touched it with his own
hand, but if someone else had used it to kill him, then how
had they got close to him without being noticed? And
where were they now?

"Chloe," I said numbly. "Can you search the building
and garden in case the person responsible is still here? I'll
call my brother."

"Of course, Head Witch," she said in a choked voice.

I unlocked the office and stumbled inside, Tansy
leaping over Malcolm's body to join me. Carmilla lay
napping in the same spot as beforehand, while Grandma's
ghost was nowhere to be seen.

"Carmilla," I called to the cat. "Carmilla. Wake up."

"This had better be good." She opened her eyes a fraction. "What is it?"

"We have another intruder, and he's dead."

"Well, that's inconvenient."

"Didn't you hear him?" asked Tansy.

"No," said Carmilla. "I heard the last one because he tried to use a spell to open the door. Who killed him?"

"Haven't a clue." He'd left the woods before all the other contenders had—and if he hadn't returned to the inn, he must have come straight here. Had he had an accomplice who'd turned against him? Or was he the person who'd brought the cursed pens here to begin with?

"Do you recognise him?" Tansy asked Carmilla. "Come and look."

"I didn't see the last intruder's face, did I?" Carmilla hopped off the desk and padded towards the doorway, peering around the corner. "I don't know him."

She wouldn't have seen most of the contenders, of course, since the only time I'd seen her leave the office was when she'd come to disrupt my conversation with Harvey yesterday. I pulled out my phone to call my brother, but a sudden loud screech came from the other side of the lobby.

Alarmed, I darted out of the office, seeing that the chicken had come waddling in from the garden and had spotted Malcolm's body. *Did Chloe let her out of the cage?*

"Dead!" screamed the chicken.

"Oh no." The last thing she needed was to see a reminder of how her witch had died, but it was too late to stop her from launching into another panicked sprint around the lobby. Tansy tried unsuccessfully to herd her back outside while I called my brother.

"Hey, Ramsey." I had to raise my voice over the chicken's screaming. "I have a dead body outside my office."

"You're joking." There was a heartbeat's pause. "I'll be right there."

The chicken disappeared into the garden with a wail of despair at the same moment as Aunt Shannon came down from the upper floor.

"Who is that?" She eyed Malcolm as if he was a misplaced textbook, not a dead body. "One of your contenders?"

"Yes, and I think he was trying to get into my office." Had she been in the building the whole time? If so, she'd surely have heard him come in, but I doubted she'd have been keeping an eye out for intruders. She'd probably been responsible for letting the chicken out of her cage too. "Didn't you hear him?"

"No, I didn't." She studied his splayed hand and the gleaming pen in his grip. "Foolish of him to attempt to strike the Head Witch."

"You don't seem shocked."

"Do you have any idea how many assassination attempts your grandmother dealt with in her time?"

"I have some idea, since she told me herself." Goose bumps prickled my arms at Aunt Shannon's calm tone. She hadn't killed him herself, had she? Vanessa couldn't be to blame, since she hadn't been here, but her mother was certainly ruthless enough. Question was, what would killing someone who'd already been disqualified from the contest achieve? Had she wanted to stop him from getting at me? Surely not. If an assassin came looking for me, she'd be more likely to give them directions than stop them.

Chloe came hurrying into the lobby again and ran upstairs. A moment later, the front door opened, and Ramsey walked in, his gaze travelling between Aunt Shannon and me before landing on the body. "Oh no."

"Don't touch the pen," I said hastily. "Unless you're sure it isn't still cursed, that is. I don't know how it ended up in his hand. None of us saw him come in."

"What about her?" Ramsey indicated Carmilla, who peered out into the lobby from behind my office door.

"She didn't hear him, and the door was locked," I said. "Chloe has gone to look for any possible intruders, but I don't know who else is in the building."

I gave Aunt Shannon a significant look, but she didn't even blink. "Nobody as far as I'm aware. Does it matter?"

"Yes, because they might have looked out the window and seen him come in." I glanced through the doors to the nearby classrooms, but I was pretty sure that if anyone had been around, the noise would have drawn their attention by now. "And his... his familiar. Where is he?"

"His familiar?" asked Ramsey. "It's that cat, right?"

"Yes, but I don't know where he is." I approached the back door, but I could only see the chicken running in circles while Tansy sat guard outside.

Chloe came hurrying downstairs, breathless. "Nobody else is upstairs."

So it was just Aunt Shannon. Why had she been here while everyone else had been watching the contest? I doubted I'd get a truthful answer from her, but before I could ask any questions, the front door opened again. This time, Mum strode in, immediately seeing Malcolm's body.

"What is going on in here?" she demanded.

"The Head Witch seems to have intercepted a potential assassin," said Aunt Shannon.

"I found him like this," I corrected her. "Outside my office. He never got inside. Aunt Shannon was the only other person in the building at the time, as far as I'm aware, but I need to find his missing familiar."

"Where's *your* familiar?" Mum asked.

"Keeping an eye on the chicken. She freaked out when she saw the body." I faced Aunt Shannon. "Did you unlock her cage?"

"Why would I do such a thing?" she asked.

Ramsey cleared his throat. "Can you all stop crowding me, please? This is a crime scene. I'll call in the rest of my team, and we have to get rid of that pen."

And find his familiar.

"Where are you going?" Mum said to Aunt Shannon, who'd made a move towards the front door. "Stay here in case we need your input."

With her and Ramsey already competing for authority, I didn't need to throw my broomstick in as well. Instead, I went to talk to Chloe. "Did you find him?"

"No, but I found the chicken," she said.

"I know where the chicken is." I was pretty sure all the neighbours did as well. Including the Henbanes.

The Henbanes. Persephone was one of the few people I hadn't watched closely throughout the last round of the contest, which might have been a mistake. Yet she hadn't been anywhere near our headquarters when Malcolm had died.

I exited the lobby and found Tansy chasing Myrtle the magpie away from the chicken. Minty had hidden herself in a bush, but that didn't stop Myrtle from circling over-head and making derisive cawing noises.

"Not this again." I walked over to the bushes. "Go away, Myrtle. Tansy, have you seen Malcolm's cat?"

"No," she said. "Wait, is he not here?"

"Wherever he is, he might have seen the killer." I shooed the magpie away from the bush. "Myrtle, can you please stop your witch from arguing with my mother so we can find out who tried to assassinate me?"

"You think you were the intended target?" Tansy's tail began to wag. "Was it that aunt of yours?"

"If she killed Malcolm, then she did the other contenders a favour, if anything." Unless he and my aunt had been working together, but he wasn't local. Vanessa was… and so was Persephone Henbane.

I found myself approaching the fence dividing our garden from the Henbane Coven's, though I would have thought Tiffany would be keeping her distance after we'd come to blows last week over her attempts to sabotage the Head Witch ceremony.

"They talked to the press a couple of days ago and told them I was guaranteed not to last a week," I muttered to Tansy. "I never did have the chance to read their interview."

"I doubt it's worth the effort," said my familiar. "Do you think *they* might be involved?"

"Tiffany doesn't like to do her own dirty work, so maybe." Persephone had made the final four, but I doubted she'd win the contest and gain the Henbanes the prestige they so deeply craved. Whether they wanted to win or not, killing someone who'd already been elimi-nated from the contest made little sense.

I searched the garden from top to bottom, but Malcolm's cat was nowhere to be seen. Minty, meanwhile, remained hiding in the bushes and refused to come out even after the magpie went to join her master. Since she was no longer screaming, I opted to leave her out of her cage and returned to the lobby.

Ramsey had moved Malcolm's body out of the way of the doors and had also secured the pen in a container so nobody could touch it with their bare hands. While he talked to someone on the phone, Mum and Chloe stood in the corner, having a hushed conversation while Aunt Shannon talked to her own familiar.

Carmilla sat watching from the office doorway, so I approached her first. "Are you sure you didn't hear anything when Malcolm came in?"

Carmilla yawned. "I can't keep track of every tedious human who comes here."

"Well, try to keep your eyes open next time," I said. "I thought you had a vested interest in keeping me alive."

Aunt Shannon made a disparaging noise. "If she's your security, then it's no wonder an intruder got in."

"He didn't get into the office," I pointed out. "Someone killed him first. Seems a bit of an overreaction if you ask me, unless he accidentally grabbed his own cursed pen."

Where had he even got it from? Everyone had been searched prior to the contest and had even left their wands in a secure room at the town hall, Vanessa included. Aunt Shannon, though, had all manner of magical advantages at her disposal, and she'd definitely been inside the building when he'd come in… which meant that either she'd ignored his intrusion, or she'd brought him to a halt in her own way. I wouldn't lie; the thought of her protecting me was too weird to contemplate. It was far more likely that she'd shrugged and looked away when she saw him enter. As for where the pen had come from, though? I didn't know.

"Robin." Mum beckoned me over to her. "You didn't find his familiar?"

"I can't find that cat anywhere," I said. "What's the plan for the other contenders?"

"Ramsey is going to send a team to search all their rooms for more of those pens," she said. "Other than that, they've been ordered not to leave town for the time being."

"Good call," I said. "I don't see how they could possibly have smuggled something that lethal into town without being caught, though."

"There are plenty of possibilities if one is inventive enough," said Aunt Shannon. "May I ask why you insist on keeping me in here? Am I a suspect?"

"You're a potential witness," Mum said. "Especially with regard to our security."

No kidding. I should have done more than leave invisible ink on the door, but I hadn't expected anyone else to break in so soon after the last time. Nobody could have anticipated that the intruder would drop dead before anyone caught him, either.

Aunt Shannon must have known. Not that she'd admit to a thing… and it was beyond me to figure out if she'd been the one who'd seen to his premature end.

9

I'd privately hoped I might be able to get in a quick nap before the next round of the contest, but I couldn't even get any work done with Ramsey's team roaming around my office. Carmilla was napping on Chloe's desk as if there wasn't a dead body in the lobby, while Mum barked orders at anyone unlucky enough to walk past.

"Mum." I tensed as she turned her glare towards me. "I can't get anything done in here. Should I look for Malcolm's missing familiar?"

"Not alone," she said. "Also, someone needs to tell the other contenders about Malcolm's unfortunate demise."

"You want *me* to tell them?" I frowned. "They might have scattered all over town."

"I'm sure you can track them down between the two of you." She clearly wasn't in the mood to take no for an answer, so I seized on the chance to get away and left the witches' headquarters with Tansy at my heels.

"Maybe his cat went back to the inn," said Tansy. "He might not know his wizard is dead."

"I don't know. I thought they went everywhere together."

Either way, I had to break the news to the other contenders, and I had zero clue how they'd take it. Malcolm had cheated, attacked my cousin's familiar, and generally behaved unscrupulously, so I doubted he had any friends among them. Yet his death was sudden and unnerving enough that I found myself watching my back as Chloe and I walked down the road towards the town's centre.

"There's your cousin," said Chloe.

Vanessa. She strode purposefully in the direction we'd just come from. Had her mother called her in as backup?

"Vanessa." I approached her, cutting off her path. "You should know… Malcolm was murdered. His body showed up inside the coven's headquarters when I went back to my office."

She looked momentarily surprised before her expression settled back into its usual scowl. "Is there a reason you're telling me this?"

"I figured you might want to know why the police are all over our road," I said. "Also, he was found holding a cursed pen, the same as Anne was, with no obvious signs of who gave it to him."

"What's your point?" she asked. "You think one of the other contenders bumped him off?"

"Actually, your mother was the only person in the building at the time," I said. "She's talking to the police."

Vanessa's eyes narrowed. "Your brother had better not be hassling her."

More like the other way around. "If you see Malcolm's familiar, would you send him my way?"

"Fine, whatever." She sidestepped me and marched on with her hands clenched at her sides.

"That was instructive." I resumed walking, Chloe hurrying alongside me. We wouldn't find all the contenders at the inn, since Persephone Henbane wouldn't be staying there, and Rowan would have returned to the café to help her familiar.

Chloe kept pace with me as we approached the Owl's Nest. "Ah—there's Piper."

"Robin." Piper gave me a wave. "I thought you were going back to the office."

"Malcolm was murdered."

"What?" Piper looked at me with blank shock on her face. "How?"

"I found him outside my office with one of those cursed pens in his hand," I said. "His familiar is missing."

"That's bizarre." Her forehead crinkled. "Why're you here, then? To find his familiar?"

"My mother has decided that I have to tell all the other contenders the news in person," I said. "Are they all back at the inns?"

"Most of them are, I think," she said. "I'll go with you."

"Chloe," I addressed my assistant. "Can you go to the other inn and tell the guests there? Piper and I will tell everyone at the Owl's Nest."

"What?" she said. "No, I'm supposed to stay beside you at all times."

"It'll be quicker," I said. "Piper will watch my back."

"You bet," said Piper. "We'll meet you outside."

Chloe looked a little unsettled, but she nodded. "Okay."

"Malcolm was staying here." I indicated the inn as she walked away. "I need to find that cat of his. The two of them were inseparable, but I didn't find him anywhere near where he died."

"Sounds dodgy." She led the way into the Owl's Nest, a pleasant inn with a blue-carpeted lobby and a bronze-haired shifter sitting behind the front desk.

"Head Witch!" The shifter receptionist jumped to his feet when he saw me. "Can I help you?"

"Yes." I approached the desk. "I'm afraid one of your guests was involved in a tragic accident. I'm here to inform the other contenders."

His face fell. "Oh, that's terrible news. Is there anything I can do?"

"Can you tell me which room Malcolm was staying in?"

"Let me check." He consulted a book on his desk. "He was in the second dorm on the first floor."

"Thanks," I said. "My mother—ah, Lady Wildwood—will be in touch soon to let you know the next steps, I'm sure." Unless my brother's team showed up first.

Meanwhile, Piper and I went up the short staircase to the first floor. When we reached the corridor, Nolan emerged from one of the dorms with a suitcase in his hand.

"Hold on." I barred his way. "Where are you going?"

"Home," he said. "I'm out of the running. Aren't I?"

"Malcolm was murdered," I said. "We'd prefer for all the contenders to stay in town until my brother gives the all clear."

His brows shot up. "Seriously?"

"Yes," I said. "Have you seen Malcolm's cat?"

He looked troubled. "No, but I'll keep an eye out for him."

Nolan himself had been nowhere near Malcolm when he'd died, and neither had any of the other contenders, but I remained on edge when I entered the dormitory.

"Head Witch," said Patrick, spotting me. "What is it?"

I raised my voice for everyone in the room to hear. "I'm afraid Malcolm has been murdered. As of now, the contest will proceed as planned, but the police will soon be here to search your rooms."

A shocked murmur passed among the contenders.

"Was it like Anne?" someone asked.

"Yes," said Piper. "Other than that, we can't give any details. Has anyone seen his cat?"

No signs of Malcolm's missing familiar materialised, and the same happened in the dorm next door. When we left for the stairs, we found the lobby had been completely taken over by Ramsey's team. He must have sent them to scour the place for any hidden cursed pens, so Piper and I left the inn before we got bombarded with questions.

"What now?" asked Piper. "Chloe is at the other inn, I suppose, but I can't see why Malcolm's cat would have gone there instead of to his own dorm."

"He's got to be somewhere," said Tansy. "Want to search the forest?"

"That'll take a while." On the other hand, the forest was rife with potential hiding places for cursed pens as well as missing cats. I didn't believe for a minute that the killer had been foolish enough to hide them in the dormitory. "I should check in with Rowan first."

"Is she going to apologise for accusing me of hurting her familiar?" Piper rolled her eyes. "I'll come with you, but I'll wait outside."

Inside Were's My Coffee?, Rowan wasn't anywhere to be seen, but I did see Harvey sitting in the corner with a couple of friends. When he looked in my direction, I gave an awkward wave, but I didn't quite dare walk any closer in case Carmilla appeared and stabbed me in the leg again.

Seemingly unconcerned, Harvey left his table and approached me. "Hey, Robin."

"Hey," I said. "Ah—have you seen Rowan anywhere?"

"Your cousin?" he asked. "I saw her a while ago. She looked pretty upset, and she was carrying a bottle of some kind of healing formula."

"Must have been for her familiar," I explained. "He got injured in the last round of the contest."

"Oh," he said. "Sorry to hear that. Is that your brother?"

When the door opened behind me, I instinctively turned around, suppressing a groan. "Ramsey, what are you doing here?"

"I might ask you the same question, Robin," he said. "I need to talk to you."

I doubted Harvey would want to hear about the latest dead body I'd run into, so I said, "Sorry, Harvey. Talk soon?"

"Sure." He waved me off, and I ducked out of the café after my brother.

"I was checking up on Rowan," I said to Ramsey before he or Prickles could start lecturing me again. "Since her familiar was injured in the last round of the contest. Then Piper and I were going to go and look for Malcolm's missing familiar."

"I know where his cat is," said Ramsey. "He showed up at the police station when I was at your office, and because I wasn't there, nobody could understand a word he said."

What? "He knows what happened to Malcolm, then?"

"Yes, he does."

"You found the missing cat?" asked Piper, overhearing. "That'll save us some searching."

"True," I said. "I'd better go and see what he has to say. Can you tell Chloe where I am?"

"Sure," she said. "Do what you have to."

At least I wouldn't have to break the news to Malcolm's familiar, but I wished we'd known his whereabouts sooner.

Ramsey led me to the police station just down the road from the town hall. It'd been a while since I'd set foot in there, but the plain brick building hadn't changed an inch and neither had the beige wallpaper or the navy-blue carpets in the entryway. What *had* changed was the fact that my brother had his own office now, as I hadn't visited home since before he'd been promoted to the head of the local police force. I gave the cosy room an appreciative glance when we followed him in. Unlike my chaotic office space, his cabinets were neatly ordered, and not a single scrap of paper littered the neat desk. I had to admit, the décor was a bit plain, with a single abstract painting on the wall and nothing more.

Tansy ran up and down the room, peering around every corner, while Prickles climbed on top of the desk. "Have you come to remove that animal?"

"Where is he?" I jumped when a hissing sound came from underneath the desk. Crouching, I spotted the stripy cat curled up, his amber eyes glowing in the darkness. "I'm sorry for what happened to your master."

The cat shuddered. "I don't understand how he died."

"He touched a cursed pen," I said. "Did you see where he picked it up?"

"He pulled it out of his pocket."

What? "He already had it?"

That meant Aunt Shannon might not be responsible after all... while the suspect pool widened to include all the contenders who might have got close enough to slip a cursed pen into Malcolm's pocket while he wasn't paying attention.

"It wasn't his," the cat insisted.

"He got it from somewhere," said Tansy. "I thought you were his familiar. Aren't you meant to watch out for people who might attack your wizard?"

The cat's ears flattened. "How dare you imply I didn't do enough to stop his killer?"

"What was he doing outside my office to begin with?" I put in. "I found his body in the headquarters of the Wildwood Coven. Why was he there?"

The cat didn't say anything. Tansy jumped under the desk, only to recoil from his claws. "Don't point your claws at me. He wanted to speak to Robin, did he? Is that why he was there?"

"That or he wanted to break into my office," I added. "Did he try the same this morning?"

"What?" The cat blinked in apparently genuine confusion. "No. I've never been to that building before. I didn't know the office was yours."

"He didn't tell you?" I found that hard to believe.

"It's true," he insisted. "He took off as soon as the last

contest round ended and ran back to town without telling me where he was going."

"Maybe he was mad at you for attacking my cousin's familiar." I narrowed my eyes at him. "Or he wanted to explain to me in person that you both cheated."

The cat's ears flattened again. "He didn't deserve to die."

"But he did cheat," Tansy said. "Who gave him that pen, I wonder? Or was he trying to give it to the Head Witch himself?"

"It wasn't his." The cat's head drooped. "He didn't tell me why he went into that building. He just reached for his wand and pulled out that pen instead… and he died."

So he'd definitely been trying to get into my office at the time. He must have known I wasn't in, surely, which meant the odds of him not being up to mischief were low.

"When did he last check his pockets? Did you see?" I asked. "Do you know when the pen might have been slipped in there?"

"He got covered in mud in the first trial," said the cat in a tremulous voice. "Then he took off his coat when he went to shower and left it lying on the bed."

"In the dorm," I said. "I guess anyone could have got hold of it, then. Were you watching?"

"No," he said. "I went to hunt in the forest."

If he was telling the truth, then it wouldn't have been impossible for the person responsible to have slipped the pen into his pocket when he'd taken off his coat. In fact, even a nonguest might have been able to sneak in. The question was, why had they killed him? He and Anne seemingly had little in common given that she'd been new to the contests while he'd been entering for years.

"You two weren't close, were you?" asked Tansy. "It sounds to me like he went behind your back a lot."

The cat made a low keening noise. "No. He didn't. I'd have done anything to help him."

"Including cheat," I said. "You scared all the other familiars in that first round and then attacked Rowan's familiar in the last one, didn't you?"

"Was it Malcolm who told you to do that?" asked Tansy.

The cat inclined his head.

"Did he want his own team to lose?" In fact, had he been helping the other team instead? I wouldn't have thought Roxy would need it, but Vanessa would definitely take any help offered, and I didn't entirely trust Persephone Henbane either. As for Patrick, I didn't know him well enough to know if he was inclined to cheat or not.

When the cat didn't respond, I straightened upright to speak to my brother. "Did he tell you anything else?"

"No," he said. "Except that his name is Jarvis, and that he's been working hand in hand with Malcolm for years. He wouldn't admit to cheating every time, but it sounds like a hobby of theirs."

"Except that despite their mutual trust, Malcolm ran to my office after the trial without telling his familiar what he was up to." If I believed Jarvis's word, that was.

"That's not right," said Ramsey. "I know Malcolm couldn't talk directly to his familiar like you and I can, but they seemed to trust one another."

"I wondered if they might have been cheating on behalf of someone else," I said. "That's the only explanation I can think of for him attacking his own teammate."

"Why'd he come to see you, though?" he asked. "To confess?"

"He must have known I wasn't in the office at the time," I said. "If he wanted to speak to me, he could have just asked me right there and then instead of running off."

"Maybe he knew who the killer was," said Ramsey. "He might have wanted to talk to you somewhere the others wouldn't overhear."

"He has a point," Tansy said. "Maybe he figured out who killed Anne."

"When would he have done that?" It was a reasonable way to explain why someone had sneakily taken him out of the picture, except he'd also planned to break into my office. That wasn't the act of someone who feared for his life and wanted to confide the identity of a murderer to me.

"I wouldn't know," said Tansy. "But the killer might have figured it out and slipped the pen into his pocket."

That widened the pool of suspects to anyone who'd been at the inn at the time, though Malcolm himself hadn't gone back to the inn until after his brief wanderings around the forest, and he'd wasted no time in telling the other contestants what the next trial would involve. Why would one of them kill him?

"That still doesn't explain how they smuggled it into the inn," I said. "All their bags were searched, right?"

"That's right," said Ramsey. "And my team has been searching both inns thoroughly in case any more of them are hidden in a corner somewhere."

"Must have cost a fortune," I said. "Not many people can afford that many commissioned curses."

Unless the person responsible had cursed the pens

themselves, but that required a rare level of skill and expertise that few managed to master.

"Exactly," he said. "Did you read the files I gave you?"

"I did," I said. "Even if Malcolm had a history of cheating, I still don't understand who might have wanted Anne dead. She'd never even entered a contest before."

And if I'd been the intended target, then why would the killer give the pen to her instead of me? Or had Anne brought the pen herself and accidentally touched it before she'd been able to use it on me? That had been one of my initial theories, but I'd seen nothing to connect Anne and Malcolm nor any proof that they'd both dabbled in illegal curses and wanted me dead.

"My team is going to contact all the listed curse experts in the surrounding towns and see if anyone knows about those cursed pens," said Ramsey. "Theoretically, it shouldn't take too long to speak to them all, but there's no guarantee that they'll know anything. Ideally, we need this case wrapped up before everyone leaves town."

In other words, by the end of the day. Or tomorrow at the latest. No pressure.

10

The last thing I wanted to do was go back to judge the semifinal of the contest with the clock ticking on the time we had to find the killer, but at least most of the suspects would be gathered in the same place while Ramsey's team did a thorough search of the inns. I was more inclined to think they'd found a cleverer place to hide those cursed pens, like in the middle of the Wildwood, but my job was to help judge the contest, not catch a killer. According to Mum, anyway.

"The semifinalists are waiting inside there." Chloe followed me into the town hall's entryway and pointed at one of the waiting rooms. "Your mother is preparing for the semifinal round."

"Where will that round be taking place?" Nobody had given me any instructions, and the contest had frankly been the last thing on my mind after Malcolm's death and his familiar's appearance at the police station.

The oak doors at the back swung open as Mum walked in. "The next round of the contest will take place in the largest local sports field. Go and fetch the contenders, won't you, Robin?"

Chloe and I fetched the four semifinalists from the waiting room and led them out of the town hall via the back exit. Outside, we could already hear the cheering of a crowd from a nearby field which was typically used for competitive sports between academy teams. The non-broomstick-related sports, anyway, because those typically required a bigger space.

"What is that?" asked Patrick, indicating a towerlike construction sticking up from the centre of the field.

"No idea." Mum had been busy, evidently.

The rest of the contenders assembled in the stands around the arena along with the other spectators. I didn't see Rowan among them, but Piper waved at me from near Nolan in the front row, who stood with his rat at his feet and surveyed the tower with an expression that suggested he was quite glad he hadn't got through to the semifinals after all. Patrick and Persephone both looked warily at the odd-shaped tower as Mum indicated for them to take up a position on a raised platform nearby, while Roxy wore her usual expression of calm confidence, and Vanessa just looked smug.

Mum beckoned Chloe and me towards another plat-form which stood between the audience and the field. Tansy scampered ahead to sit at my feet while Mum picked up a microphone and called the chattering crowd to silence. "Welcome to the semifinal round of the Familiar Contest. Congratulations to our finalists: Patrick Wellman, Vanessa Wildwood, Roxy Denton, and Perse-phone Henbane."

Cheering ensued from the crowd before petering out into silence.

"This round will decide the finalists," Mum said. "The goal is simply to climb that tower—both humans and familiars. The two who reach the top first will advance to the final. The other two will be pitted against one another for third and fourth place."

Tension zipped through the arena as the meaning sank in. This was it. This round would decide the layout of the rest of the contest, in which one of the four contenders wouldn't get a prize at all, while the others would all win trophies.

Mum waved her wand, and lights sprang up around the tower so that we could all see it more clearly. Up close, the contraption resembled an adult fun house, with ladders and climbing walls and nets. The familiars would have an easier time navigating their way through, especially the ones who could fly, but their owners had to reach the top as well.

"I wish I could join in," Tansy said. "That looks like so much fun."

"Maybe you can ask Mum if you can have a go when this contest round is over."

The four contenders and their familiars gathered at the starting line around the base of the tower.

"Everyone ready?" Mum gave me a nod, indicating to me to start the round.

I raised the sceptre. "Begin."

The bird familiars took flight first, but their companions weren't so lucky. As soon as the contenders began to climb the tower, a series of bizarre special effects disrupted them, from sudden showers of rain to blinding sunlight and patches of darkness which prevented them from seeing where they were going.

Tansy and I both burst out laughing when the rain caused Vanessa to slide backwards down a slope and land on her rear at the bottom. Her familiar flew above her head, but the little bird wasn't strong enough to help her climb.

"Look at her face," Tansy snickered.

"Is Aunt Shannon here?" I didn't see her in the crowd, so I trod closer to Mum and whispered the same question to her. She shook her head without elaborating, and I wished I'd opted out of watching the contest's final rounds. The last time I'd seen Aunt Shannon was when she and Mum had been arguing back at the witches' headquarters, and she'd never given a satisfactory explanation as to what she'd been doing in the building at the time— or why she hadn't noticed Malcolm's death.

I forced my attention back to the contest with difficulty, but impatience prickled beneath my skin. If Aunt Shannon was up to her usual mischief elsewhere in town, then someone ought to be keeping an eye on her. Hoping Ramsey had had the same thought, I watched Roxy's raven and Persephone's familiar struggle to help their owners climb the slope, while Patrick's cat had to dig his claws in to keep from sliding downhill.

Roxy reached the top first, but Vanessa moved into second place while Patrick and Persephone slid down a slope which had turned slick with rainwater. When Patrick struggled to the top, desperation flitted across Persephone's face as she slid back down the slope again.

If I hadn't been watching her, I might not have heard

her panicked voice as she called to her familiar. "Help me find a shortcut!"

The little bird flew around her head and squeaked. "Turn left!"

When I squinted through the sheen of rain, I saw the route to the left did indeed lead to a shortcut up to the next level of the path. Persephone turned that way, relief etched on her features, while suspicion trickled down my spine. Her familiar had told her where to go, but he hadn't given any nonverbal cues. She shouldn't have been able to understand his speech.

Persephone's shortcut enabled her to overtake both Patrick and Vanessa, causing her to close in behind Roxy on her way to the top. Roxy maintained a clear lead, and a cheer rose up from the crowd when she and her raven reached the tower's peak.

My heart sank when Persephone joined her within minutes. She'd won her way to the final... but had she cheated in the process? I edged closer to Mum. "Did you hear that?"

"Hear what?"

"Persephone understood her familiar when he spoke," I said. "He told her where to take a shortcut to the top, but he didn't give any nonverbal cues."

She tilted her head in my direction. "Are you sure?"

"Almost certain." I'd definitely heard him speak, but I wouldn't have guessed she'd understood if she hadn't followed his instructions directly. Her familiar hadn't used gestures to tell her where to go.

"She definitely cheated." Tansy climbed up my shoulder. "I heard it too."

"She doesn't have our family's gift, though," I said. "She's a Henbane witch."

"The round is over," Mum said in a low voice. "If I'm to make an accusation, I need proof."

"Can't you hold off on the announcement for the next round?" I asked. "If she cheated, then she might not be the only person who did. Is there another interlude before the final rounds?"

"Yes, there is," she said. "With that being said, it's not possible for me to delay."

What was that supposed to mean? She wanted to save face, I knew, but I should have expected trickery from a Henbane witch. "I get it, but—"

Mum's voice rang out across the arena. "Everyone is to leave while I get the arena ready for the final round. All contenders have half an hour to prepare. Use it wisely."

As she waved her wand, the tower reverted to the pile of stacked boxes it had originally consisted of, and the contenders were able to climb back to steady ground. The audience began to disperse, and Piper moved over to our platform.

"Hey, Robin," she said. "Is it just me, or was that Persephone talking to her familiar?"

"Yes," I said in an undertone. "I think she was cheating, but I'm not sure how she made her familiar able to understand her."

"A spell or a potion, I'd guess," she said. "Nobody has their wands, even the disqualified contenders. Right?"

"Not that I'm aware of," I said. "It's possible another Henbane Coven member gave her a potion or used a spell secretly."

Ramsey was searching the rooms at the inn, but Persephone was local, and so was the rest of her coven.

"What do you want me to do?" Piper asked. "If she's cheating, she ought to be disqualified."

"Is Tiffany Henbane somewhere in the audience?" I asked. "Because she's known for bending the rules on behalf of her coven."

"Yes, she is," said Piper. "Want me to hex her?"

"No, I just want to talk to her." The crowd continued to disperse through the doors to the town hall. It'd be easier to talk to Persephone herself, preferably before the next round started, but she seemed in no hurry to get down from the remains of the tower.

Vanessa hopped to the ground and gave me a derisive look as if daring me to mock her for losing out on the top prize. Patrick followed soon after, picking up his cat familiar to carry him out of the arena. The two would face one another in the next round, but if Persephone was a cheat, then he and Vanessa ought to be in the top three by default.

Assuming he hadn't cheated too.

Chloe cleared her throat from beside me. "I couldn't help overhearing what you said. Are you sure you want to make an accusation against the Henbanes?"

"Not without proof, but they're known for under-handed tactics." They also had good reason to want me out of my position as Head Witch. "Don't say anything to them just yet. I'm going to speak to the others."

As Patrick left the arena, I stepped off the platform and caught up with him as he made his way to the exit. "Hey. Can I have a word?"

"Sure." He halted by the exit, his cat in his arms, wearing a questioning look on his face.

"I have reason to believe Persephone was bending the rules." I kept my voice low. "Did you hear her speak to her familiar?"

"No." He stiffened. "She cheated? Really?"

"I'm sure she did," I said, "but I've yet to figure out how she made herself capable of understanding her familiar. If you know anything, it would be helpful if you let me know."

He shook his head. "It's none of my business."

"You won't get into trouble." I dropped my voice. "We're looking for a murderer, too, so the cheating takes a back seat. That said, if we find proof she cheated, you'll automatically be in the top three contenders. So will Vanessa."

His lips pressed together, and I could see the thoughts ticking over in his mind. "You won't tell anyone I told you?"

"I won't," I said. "I just want to know the truth."

He took a deep breath. "I saw Persephone drinking from a potion bottle outside the town hall before this round started. She thought she was alone, I think."

"Do you know where she got it?"

"No." A slight pause followed. "But I saw her talking to Malcolm this morning outside the inn. They looked like they didn't want to be overheard."

Malcolm. Maybe there was a link between his death and the contest after all. "Thanks. That really helps."

I let him leave the arena while I waited for Persephone to climb down the tower.

"I should have known she was cheating," Tansy said. "That Malcolm too. I bet he took that potion himself."

"So he and his familiar could understand one another." Why, then, had he not confided in his familiar when he'd come to my office? I definitely needed to talk to Jarvis the cat again, but that would have to wait until after I confronted Persephone. Now that I thought about it, it was just like the Henbanes to hire someone to ensure their victory. Was she the one who'd convinced Malcolm to disrupt the last round in order to guarantee her team got through to the semifinals?

I waited for Roxy and her raven to leave before going to meet Persephone at the foot of the tower. "I know what you did."

I meant to take her off guard. It worked, because she gave a violent start. "I don't know what you mean."

"If I search the bins outside the town hall, will I find an empty bottle of a potion which enabled you to talk to your familiar?"

She went pink. "What?"

"Come on, we'll both look." I made to leave, and her expression crumpled.

"Please don't kick me out of the contest," she whispered.

"If you didn't want to get kicked out, you shouldn't have cheated," I said. "Who gave you the potion? You bought it from somewhere."

She shook her head. "I brought it myself."

She was a terrible liar, really. I studied her face, the way she bit her lip and avoided my eyes. "Did you give any to the other contenders?"

Another headshake. "No."

"It was Malcolm who gave it to you, wasn't it?"

At his name, she blinked hard and looked away. "No."

"I know he was cheating, too," I said. "If he offered the same potion to the other contenders, I need to know. It's only fair."

"I don't know." She squeezed her eyes shut. "He approached me with the potion and gave it to me for free. That's all."

"Why'd he do that?" For free? A likely story. Why she'd feel compelled to defend him, though, I hadn't a clue.

She shrugged one shoulder. "He knew I wanted to win."

There must be more to it than that, surely. "Did he offer it to any of the others?"

"He might have, but I didn't see."

I'd have to ask the others individually, and at the moment, we were the only people left in the arena except for Mum and Chloe. The latter came hurrying over when I beckoned to her.

"Chloe," I said. "Please escort Persephone Henbane to another room for questioning."

"What?" Persephone flinched. "I didn't kill him. Malcolm, I mean. I really didn't."

"We need you to answer a few questions, right, Chloe?"

"Right." She beckoned for Persephone to follow her, while I went into the lobby and found Piper waiting with Ramsey.

"Robin," he said. "Piper said someone was cheating."

"Persephone Henbane drank a potion which enabled her to understand her familiar." I gestured towards her bowed head as Chloe led her into one of the waiting rooms. "Allegedly, Malcolm gave it to her before he died. As a favour."

"I see," he said. "You think that's why someone killed him?"

"Might be." Why he'd shown up at my office was another matter entirely, but if he made a habit of giving away free potions to help people cheat, it explained why he always ranked in the top eight but never won.

The question was, what was he gaining out of the cheating if he wasn't winning prizes?

Ramsey watched Chloe shut the door on Persephone, trapping her in the waiting room. "Her aunt isn't going to be happy."

"Is it really that surprising that one of the Henbanes was cheating?" I asked. "If this is serial behaviour on Malcolm's part, though, it's not a stretch to imagine he might have annoyed someone enough for them to want him dead."

Was Persephone the killer? Surely not, given that he'd helped her, but if he'd made the same offer to others, then they might not have been pleased to end up eliminated. I was still missing a few pieces of this puzzle, though.

Why did he come to my office? Was he there to confess... or to warn me?

Ramsey went to search the bins around the town hall for the potion bottle Persephone had been drinking from, while Piper raised a brow at the sound of her loud protests from behind the closed door. "She's not happy."

"*Did* you see Tiffany in the audience?"

"I thought I did," she said. "But she slipped away before I could get close enough to find her."

"Also, have you seen Aunt Shannon?" I asked. "She wasn't around either."

"No, I haven't," she said. "Wait, wasn't she near your office during the break-in?"

"Precisely why I'd like to know where she is." I looked over to the back door as Mum entered the lobby. "Persephone is in that room over there waiting to be questioned. Ramsey's looking for the potion bottle she threw out."

"She did cheat, then?" Mum asked.

"Yes, but she got the potion from Malcolm," I said.

"Before he died. And she doesn't know if he made the same offer to any of the other contenders."

"In other words, everyone's a suspect again," said Piper. "Should I feel insulted that he didn't make the offer to me?"

"Maybe he knew you were reporting to me behind the scenes," I said. "I wonder if he approached Rowan."

"Or Vanessa."

Mum's eyes narrowed. "You can try asking her but I doubt he did. Not if he knows that she can already understand her familiar."

"True," I said. "Still, I can't help wondering what he hoped to achieve by giving those potions away for free."

"Not much of a business model," said Piper.

"Tell me about it." I shook my head. "Maybe he had one particular candidate he wanted to win… there he is."

Ramsey reentered the lobby, holding a grimy-looking bottle in his hand. "I found this, but it's not the only one. My team reported finding at least three similar bottles in the bins around the centre of Wildwood Heath."

"So this was widespread," I said. "Other contenders used the same potion."

"Everyone's a suspect, like I said," Piper said.

"Nevertheless, if Persephone is disqualified, that means we have only three remaining candidates for the final round," Mum said. "I'll have to adapt the contest accordingly if we can't divide them into pairs."

"Unless we pick someone from the last round…" With Malcolm dead, though, I doubted anyone would want to volunteer, except perhaps Piper. "I guess there isn't a fair way to do that."

"No, there isn't," Mum said. "Where is Persephone Henbane?"

"In the waiting room, with Chloe supervising her." I could hear the faint sound of sobbing on the other side of the door. "Ramsey wants to question her first, right?"

I had the feeling she'd already told me everything she planned to, but I'd rather she didn't go wandering off when I hadn't ruled out her involvement in the murders yet. There was the rest of her coven to consider, too, and it seemed odd that she'd accepted a free potion from a stranger rather than asking for their help instead.

"Who *isn't* a suspect?" Piper asked. "Except for me and Rowan?"

"Patrick," I said. "He told me that he saw Persephone drinking the potion, but I don't think he did anything dodgy himself. There's also Vanessa…"

"I saw her outside," Ramsey said. "I'm going to talk to Persephone first."

"I'll find Vanessa." I turned to Mum. "How are we going to decide who else to question about the potions? Or should we save the questioning until after the contest?"

"We'll speak to the other finalists first," she said decisively. "The rest can wait until afterwards, unless we have substantial evidence. We can't let the contest go off the rails at this stage."

"Malcolm was murdered, though," I said. "What if a dissatisfied client was the person who did it?"

"The only way to find out is to talk to everyone," said Piper. "Let's snag Vanessa to start off with."

I led the way out of the town hall, spotting Vanessa

pacing along the road with her familiar on her shoulder. At a guess, nobody else wanted to talk to her.

When I approached her, she said, "What?"

"Persephone got kicked out for cheating," I said bluntly. "That means the final round will have a few changes."

She barely blinked. "And?"

"Where's your mother?"

"Who wants to know? I don't see why that's any of your business."

"Considering the last time I saw her was next to Malcolm's dead body outside my office," I said, "then I'd say it *is* my business. What's she up to?"

"You think she put a curse on your contenders?" She rolled her eyes. "Not likely."

I didn't think it *was* Aunt Shannon, not this time, but there was something ugly at work behind the scenes that went beyond a few potions. I had a hard time believing Vanessa had known nothing at all.

"Forget that, then," I said. "Did Malcolm offer you a free potion?"

"A what?" She blinked. "Wow, you're really stretching to find a reason to kick me out."

"Persephone Henbane was given a potion by Malcolm that enabled her to understand her familiar," I said. "I know you don't need one of those, but we found evidence that she wasn't the only one who took him up on the offer. Did you hear him make the offer to anyone else?"

"No, because I wasn't staying at the inn," she said. "I do live here, in case you've forgotten. And he wouldn't have had a reason to offer anything to me. You'll have to try harder if you want me gone."

Without another word, she turned and walked away, her familiar flitting behind her.

"Do you want me to go after her?" asked Piper.

"No need," I said. "Malcolm probably knew there was no point in making the offer to Vanessa."

Whether we liked each other or not didn't even come into it. She wasn't a worthy target.

"Maybe, but she might have seen him talking to one of the others."

"They'll be questioned separately regardless," I said. "I just need to talk to the finalists… and Roxy is the only one we haven't already questioned."

"She's over there." Piper pointed across the street towards the coffee shop, where Roxy stood, feeding something to her raven. "Want to do this now?"

"No time to waste." I strode over to Roxy, who greeted me with a nod.

"Head Witch," she said.

"Hey," I said. "I thought you ought to know that Persephone Henbane was just disqualified for cheating."

"Cheating?" She raised her brows. "What did she do?"

"She drank a potion which enabled her to understand her familiar's speech," I said. "It turns out Malcolm gave it to her, and she wasn't the only contender he made the offer to. Did he offer you the same?"

I'd thought she was playing by the rules, but I found it hard to believe that she didn't know about his unscrupulous behind-the-scenes dealings.

"Yes," she said. "He made me the offer."

"And?" I pressed. "Did you accept?"

"No." Her answer was sure, confident, but when Tansy

climbed onto my shoulder to get a closer look at her raven, he ruffled his feathers in a discomfited manner.

"Has he done this before?" I asked. "You two have both entered quite a few contests together. He's never ranked higher than the top eight, but I assume this isn't his first time manipulating the results."

She gave her raven a stroke. "He's made me the same offer before, but I've never accepted."

"You didn't turn him in?"

She lowered her gaze. "I always thought he'd get caught."

She'd managed to win the last three contests without his help, but the fact that she'd let him get away unpunished didn't sit right with me.

"Did you see him make the offer to anyone else?" asked Piper.

"No," she said. "I think he approached each person individually."

"Makes sense," I said. "Is that why his familiar sometimes attacked the other animals?"

"I don't know," she said. "We've never really spoken much."

"My brother might want to question you anyway," I warned. "He's talking to Persephone right now. We found evidence that several other contenders accepted help from Malcolm, so we need to find out who they were."

"I'll be sure to let you know if I find out," said Roxy. "I'm sorry I didn't tell you sooner."

For the first time, her composure appeared somewhat shaken as Piper and I left her behind and returned to the town hall.

"She didn't accept his offer," said Piper. "I thought not. She's good enough that she doesn't need to cheat."

"She's known about this for years, though."

Malcolm's record went back so far that I had to wonder why he hadn't been caught yet. Had the person who'd killed him been intending to dispense justice in their own way? Maybe, but a dissatisfied former client was only one possibility. The killer's trail might still lead us back to Aunt Shannon.

Ramsey was waiting in the town hall's entryway when we returned. "Did you talk to the other finalists?"

"Vanessa wasn't offered the potion," I said. "Roxy was, but she refused. This seems to be a habit of his, though."

"And she never reported him," Piper added. "She's over at the café if you want to call her in."

"I'm not sure there's anything else she didn't already tell us," I said. "I think she was concerned about drawing the attention of the killer if she said too much."

"Aren't we all?" Piper said. "I mean, I assume I'm not the only person concerned about someone slipping a cursed pen into my pocket."

"No, you aren't." Chloe closed the door on the waiting room and came to join us. "Head Witch, what do you need me to do now?"

"Gather the other contenders." I nodded to Ramsey. "Or rather, suspects. I'm not sure how you want to organise the questioning. It might be easier if you ask each person if they were offered the potion and then invite them to come for a private chat if they have more information."

"Not when they're scattered around the middle of town," he said.

"You can ask the rest of your team to round everyone up, can't you?" I asked. "They can't have wandered that far."

"I can help," said Piper. "I think I can convince the other contenders to admit if they were offered the potion."

Ramsey's expression turned conflicted. "You don't work for the police."

"I'll do the same," I put in. "Come on, we need to get this sorted before the final round, right? We have less than half an hour."

"More like fifteen minutes." He exhaled in a sigh. "All right, fine. Tell anyone who has information on the potion to wait in the spare room."

Chloe insisted on tailing me outside, but I didn't mind having backup when I went in search of the other contenders. Piper, Ramsey, and the rest of his team split up to do the same, with the result that we soon assembled a small group of people consisting of a mixture of those who'd been eliminated in the preliminary round of the contest and those who'd been knocked out of the running earlier that day. Some denied having been approached by Malcolm outright, but enough people admitted to speaking to him that the others gradually gained the nerve to make a confession. By the time my brother and I met back at the town hall, we had more than two dozen people crowded into the spare room.

I addressed the assembled contenders. "Were you all approached by Malcolm, who made you the offer of a potion to help give you an edge in the contest?"

Heads nodded, and everyone looked uncomfortable.

"How many of you have more information about the

offer he gave you?" I asked. "Did he offer you the potion for free?"

More nods. Yet for all his industriousness, Malcolm seemingly hadn't told anyone his reasons for helping the others cheat.

"Who's entered a contest alongside Malcolm before?" I asked. "Raise your hands."

A few hands went up.

"How many of you were aware of Malcolm's habit of giving away potions to contenders?"

A couple of hands went down, but most stayed up. So Roxy was far from the only person who'd kept his secret.

"Those of you with your hands up are to go with Ramsey for further questioning," I said. "You aren't being arrested, but we're trying to get to the bottom of what Malcolm was doing before he died."

As I joined Ramsey to help with the individual questionings, we received similar answers from each person he spoke to. Most had been offered the potion, if not during this contest, then during a previous one. He'd also targeted lots of first-time entrants judging by the number of people who'd come forward who hadn't been involved in previous contests.

During a gap between the questionings, Ramsey checked the time. "The others will be on their way back to the arena now."

"I know," I said. "Is it bad that I don't really care who wins? Roxy and Patrick both got the offer from Malcolm and never reported him, and Vanessa is… Vanessa."

"I can send you a report later," he said. "That's what I did for Grandma whenever she had to deal with people cheating in contests she supervised."

"It's happened before?"

"Nobody has died until now," he said hastily. "But cheating… yes, it's more common than you'd think. So is contenders refusing to tell tales on one another."

"They're not making it easy to find out who killed him."

"I'm not so sure the person who killed Malcolm was in the circle of people he gave those potions to," said Ramsey. "And if they were, then that wasn't their only motive. He wouldn't have had time to offer Anne the potion before she died, would he? So why kill her as well as him?"

"Good question." I'd nearly forgotten her and that ridiculous chicken, who I assumed was still hiding in a bush back at the witches' headquarters. "I wish I'd been in my office when Malcolm tried to break in. Then I might have caught him out before he died."

"Not necessarily," he said. "He wouldn't have chosen to confide in you if you weren't overseeing the contest."

I frowned. "You think he was going to turn himself in?"

Which would still implicate a dissatisfied customer as the killer, but that still left Anne's death as a complete mystery. She'd arrived late to the contest, and I was pretty sure she and Malcolm hadn't spoken a word to one another.

"There's a fair possibility," said Ramsey. "That said, I don't typically use hunches to make my decisions. I look at the facts and motives."

"We have plenty of possible motives," I said. "But we need to take another look at the facts. How did Malcolm hide all these potions without being found out? Someone must have been covering for him. That or he found a really secure hiding spot."

His brow furrowed. "You make a fair point. We searched all the dorms at both inns, and we didn't find any other potions. None of those pens, either."

My thoughts went back to Malcolm's cat. "Has Jarvis said anything else? I'm sure he knows more than he told us about why Malcolm came to my office."

"I might be able to understand his speech, but I can't make him talk," he said. "We're keeping him at the police station for now, since it's safer than letting him roam around. Is that chicken still at your office?"

"She was hiding in a bush in the garden the last I saw," I said. "I don't trust Aunt Shannon or her familiar, though."

Instinct told me to go and look for her, but I had an obligation to show up at the contest, and I had yet to figure out how to use the sceptre to create a clone to attend instead of me. In fact, I hadn't got the chance to practise using it at all.

The door opened, and Mum came into the waiting room. "How is the questioning going?"

"We found out Malcolm offered the potions to most of the contenders," I said. "Not all of them accepted, but I think it's easier to ask who *didn't* get the offer from him at this stage. But he didn't ask for money, and nobody seems to know what he had to gain."

"The final round is starting in five minutes, Robin," Mum said.

"I know. I'm coming." I rose to my feet. "Ramsey, let me know if you learn anything else."

Mum didn't say another word until we reached the

doors at the back of the town hall. "Robin, you need to leave the investigation to Ramsey. It's his job, not yours."

"Excuse me?" She chose *now* to stonewall me? "I know I'm Head Witch, but I might be the killer's target. I'm not sold on this simply being a grudge from a dissatisfied customer."

"Nevertheless," she said. "If the Head Witch finds herself under threat, it's customary for her not to take a direct role in the investigation."

"So you don't want me to delegate paperwork, but you want me to turn my back on a threat to my life?" Unbelievable. "The contest is almost over. Once it's done, we'll lose our shot at cornering the killer."

"Let Chloe keep an eye out for threats," she said. "That's her job."

"She's my assistant. I won't ask her to take a bullet for me." Or cursed pen, as it were. Besides, I was so close to putting the pieces of the puzzle together. I was happy to leave Ramsey in charge of the questioning while I played the role of Head Witch, but the final round of the contest might be the killer's last chance to reach me.

One way or another, this was where it would end.

12

Mum and I reentered the arena for the final round of the contest and climbed onto the same platform as before while the crowd filed back into the seats around the arena to watch. This time, three separate platforms stood at intervals across the grassy field, one for each contender to stand on, and a considerable number of mutters and stares ensued when the audience noticed there were only three platforms, no doubt wondering where the fourth contender was.

Mum called everyone to attention. "Welcome to the final round of the Familiar Contest. As you might have noticed, there's been a change of arrangements for the final round, but I'm sure the contenders will be happy to adapt."

A questioning murmur passed through the audience before fading to silence.

Mum went on: "Persephone Henbane has been disqualified for cheating."

This time, shock reverberated through the crowd, and Mum waited for silence before continuing.

"That said, the other three contenders will still be taking part in an altered version of the final round." said Mum. "Congratulations to Patrick Wellman, Roxy Denton, and Vanessa Wildwood."

Cheering rose as the three remaining contenders entered the arena, waiting behind a line which had been painted on the grass near the platforms.

"There will be one final round, not two, and all three contenders will receive a prize no matter how they fare in this trial," Mum said. "When the Head Witch gives the signal, each of you is to climb onto the platform which corresponds to your starting point. The aim of this round is simply to be the last person standing. If either you or your familiar falls off the platform, then both of you lose by default. The last to remain standing will be declared the victor."

Another murmur travelled through the audience. When Mum nodded to me, I raised the sceptre into the air. "Begin."

The three contenders climbed onto the platforms, as did their familiars. The instant they did, Mum raised her wand, and the three platforms rose like towers, trembling as though an earthquake shook the ground underfoot. Light ignited Mum's wand as she sent various spells at the contenders in an attempt to knock them off the platforms. The crowd roared and cheered throughout, eager to see who would come out on top.

Tansy nudged me in the arm. "Is she supposed to be here?"

"Who?" I squinted past the platforms, and my heart

plunged when I heard a distinct squawking noise amid the sound of the cheering crowd. Then a bundle of feathers ran onto the grass, heading straight for our platform.

What is she doing?

I waved and called to the chicken, "Get over here!"

The chicken ignored me. She probably couldn't hear over the sound of the audience, though I heard some laughter from behind me as they caught on to the intruder's presence. Who'd let her in here? I moved to the edge of the platform and spotted someone who definitely *hadn't* been present at the start of the final round. *Aunt Shannon.*

"Robin," Mum hissed at me as I made to climb off the platform and into the audience. "What are you doing?"

"Getting that chicken out of here." I dropped to the ground before she or Chloe could stop me, Tansy clinging to my shoulder as I ducked through the audience. Unfortunately, there wasn't any way to hide the fact that I had the sceptre, so everyone knew the Head Witch was on the move, including Aunt Shannon herself.

The chicken, meanwhile, ran in panicked circles below the contenders' platforms, seemingly oblivious to the contest taking place. I hadn't a hope of reaching her from the audience, so I skirted the crowd until I caught up to Aunt Shannon near the exit. "What are you doing?"

"Me?" She arched a brow. "Watching my daughter, of course."

"You think I don't know your familiar has been taunting that chicken all day?" I whispered. "You brought her here, didn't you?"

"You think I'm to blame for that ridiculous bird interrupting the contest?" she said. "I'm not the person who let it loose in the garden."

"I'll get her." Tansy jumped off my shoulder and streaked into the arena. A red squirrel was even more noticeable than a chicken, and the crowd's attention followed her bright tail as she sprinted across the grass and attempted to herd the chicken towards the exit. As she did so, Patrick fell off his platform and tumbled over on the grass.

"You seriously did *this* for Vanessa to win the contest?" I hissed at Aunt Shannon. "That's low, even for you."

"The bird left the garden of her own accord," she replied. "See? Here she comes."

The chicken came barrelling towards the exit with Tansy in close pursuit. Aunt Shannon seized the chance to vanish among the crowd, while I waved goodbye to the last shreds of my dignity and ran after my familiar. The chicken continued to flee, wings pumping, ignoring Tansy's attempts to grab her from behind.

"Get back here!" I called after her.

The chicken ignored me, pelting through the back doors of the town hall and straight through the lobby. If she got into the main part of town, she might well take off into the forest again. I had to catch her first.

Tansy caught up to her, but all she managed to do was pull out a few feathers before Minty escaped her grasp and sprinted off. Panic gripped me. "Stop!"

The chicken didn't so much as slow down. A fresh wave of alarm hit me when she veered close to the coffee shop. Raising the sceptre, I cast an immobilising charm. A flash of light went off, brighter than I'd expected, and the chicken keeled over at once.

"Now you've done it," said Tansy. "Or should I say, *over*done it."

I hurried over to the chicken. "Oh no."

The chicken wasn't moving at all. Why had I used the sceptre and not my wand? I tucked the sceptre under my arm before I crouched down and scooped her up in my arms, which felt like picking up a feathery statue rather than a living bird. At least she'd stopped trying to escape, if nothing else.

"I need to put her somewhere secure." I paced down the road. "Maybe the police station…"

"Ramsey will be thrilled to have a chicken statue to go with his new cat," said Tansy.

"Don't even." While most people were watching the final round of the contest, I saw a few faces staring at me from inside the café. A flush heated my face as I walked over to the automatic doors to the police station.

The receptionist goggled at the sight of the Head Witch carrying a chicken into the police station. "Your brother is questioning some suspects."

Ramsey emerged from behind a door a moment later, as if he'd detected my presence through some brotherly sixth sense. "What are you doing with that chicken?"

"She interrupted the contest," I said. "I think Aunt Shannon's familiar chased her across town."

"What's wrong with her?" He strode over to peer down at the bird. "Is she frozen?"

"I used an immobilising spell," I said. When he raised a brow, I added, "With the sceptre."

"Robin." He sighed. "Really."

"She was running amok outside. I didn't have many options." I held out the chicken. "Can you keep an eye on her? I need to find Aunt Shannon, and she's hidden herself among the crowd."

"I'm sure our mother will be watching her."

"She won't," I said. "She's too focused on the contest. Which suspects are you questioning?"

"Persephone Henbane," he said. "She didn't answer all my questions to my satisfaction, so I brought her here. I couldn't help noticing that Tiffany Henbane has yet to show up to defend her niece."

"She's not at the arena either." I frowned. "She must know her niece got kicked out for cheating by now."

"Is the final round still in progress?"

"Last I checked."

At this point, I hardly cared who won. Vanessa would get a shiny trophy one way or another, but her mother's underhanded tactics reminded me that I still had yet to wrangle a decent set of answers from the chicken as to whether Anne had been in any way connected to Malcolm's schemes or to his death. "Can I leave Minty in your office?"

He blew out a frustrated breath. "Fine, but I'm not letting any other wayward familiars into my office."

"I'm guessing that doesn't include me?" Tansy scampered ahead and pushed open the door to Ramsey's office while I carried the chicken through and placed her on the desk.

"What are you doing?" Ramsey asked when I raised the sceptre over her frozen body.

"Undoing this spell." I gave the sceptre a wave, but the chicken simply drifted a couple of inches across the desk and didn't stir. "Maybe not."

"You used a simple immobilising spell?" Ramsey

stepped behind me. "They generally wear off on their own."

"Not sure this one will." I tried again, but the chicken didn't budge an inch.

Ramsey pulled out his wand. "I'll see if I can undo it, then."

Movement stirred under the desk, and Malcolm's familiar stuck his head out. He then withdrew when I crouched down to talk to him.

"Hey," I said. "Jarvis, isn't it? I heard your master had quite the business operation going on."

The cat said nothing.

"He won't talk," said Ramsey. "I tried asking about the potions, and he mysteriously lost his ability to communicate."

"Let me try." I moved onto my knees to make it easier to see the stripy cat sitting beneath the desk. "I found out Malcolm was giving potions to the other contenders to enable them to speak to their familiars. Did he ever take one himself?"

The cat didn't answer.

"It sounds like he's been doing the same thing for years," I went on. "Did you help him?"

Tansy hopped down to speak to Jarvis. "I know he was your partner, but if one of his customers wanted him dead, don't you want to know who it was?"

"Nobody knows." His tail twitched with unhappiness. "I don't know who killed Malcolm. It might have been any of them."

"Or none of them." Another thought occurred to me. "Did he offer a potion to Anne?"

"No," he said. "He didn't."

It didn't surprise me, given her late arrival to the contest, but what had put her on the killer's radar? And if there wasn't a connection, had he found *her* killer and paid for that discovery with his life? I had a hard time believing he was entirely innocent, but I had yet to find any proof that his business had been connected to the murderer, whoever it was.

A flash of light from Ramsey's wand made me rise to my feet, but the chicken remained immobile on the desk. "You did a thorough job with that spell, Robin."

"Wish I'd done the same to Aunt Shannon." My hands clenched at the thought of her smugly watching the contest at the arena as if she hadn't purposefully tried to undermine me in front of the audience.

Ramsey put his wand away. "I'm sure the spell will wear off eventually."

"It's supposed to last for five seconds, not hours." So much for the chicken calming down enough to answer my questions. "Though it would come in handy if I used it on the killer."

His brows rose. "The Head Witch isn't supposed to endanger her life. Mum was right... I never should have invited you to help with the questioning."

I gave him a hard stare. "It's one thing asking me not to intervene in a murder investigation, but if I'm the killer's target, then I ought to be allowed to defend myself."

His gaze broke away. "I don't make the rules."

"They aren't rules." Taking a back seat had made sense for Grandma, who'd been over ninety by the time she'd died, but if someone wanted me dead, I wanted to confront them directly. Hiding wasn't my style, and neither was forcing someone else to take the hit on my behalf. Admittedly, I'd left Chloe behind when I'd sprinted out of the arena, but she was my assistant, not my bodyguard.

Speaking of the arena, it was a safe bet the contest would be over by this point, and Mum would be furious if I didn't come back to congratulate the winner.

Ramsey exhaled in a sigh as I made for the door. "Where are you going?"

"To find out who won." *And corner Aunt Shannon before she slips away.*

As I left the police station, I heard a loud roar from the field behind the town hall.

"I think it's over," Tansy remarked.

I broke into a sprint, glad that I'd at least caught the chicken and had something to show for my absence. Upon reaching the arena, I slowed my pace to make my way through the crowd, cheers echoing from the spectators. My heart gave an unpleasant jolt when I spotted Vanessa standing in the centre of her platform, beaming, her familiar sitting on her shoulder. *She won?*

"The winner," Mum said from her platform, "is Vanessa Wildwood and her familiar, Hector."

Vanessa had won. Whether it was entirely due to her mother's antics, I couldn't say, but Patrick and Roxy both stood on the grass below, looking dejected. Especially Roxy. How had she managed to lose to Vanessa of all people? Had she thrown the match on purpose out of guilt over not reporting Malcolm? Or had she been distracted by the interrogation? Questions swirled around my head, and it wasn't until I heard Aunt Shannon loudly boasting, "That's my daughter!" that I spotted her amid the spectators.

She'd also seen me, but the crowd thickened around her as everyone went to offer their congratulations. I had zero chance of getting her alone to question her yet, so I continued to make my way through the audience until I reached the platform where Mum and Chloe stood.

Bracing myself, I climbed onto the platform and whispered to Mum, "I caught the chicken. She's with Ramsey."

"I'm glad you didn't humiliate both of us for nothing." Her words were sharp as hailstones, and without waiting for a reply, she spoke into the microphone "The Head Witch would like to say a few words."

No, she wouldn't. Yet despite the ongoing cheers, the crowd's attention turned to me.

"Congratulations to Vanessa Wildwood." The fact that I managed to say those words with a straight face was prizeworthy in itself. "All three winners will receive their prizes at the trophy ceremony, which starts this evening at seven." I assumed *that* hadn't changed, at least.

The crowd's cheering rose in volume. Vanessa basked in the attention, while Aunt Shannon remained surrounded by a throng of admirers. It seemed she had no intention of letting me corner her.

Mum glowered at me. "You left the bird with Ramsey, did you?"

"Yes, I did," I said. "Look, I'm sorry I ran out on you, but you can't pretend that chicken wasn't a major distraction. I'm sure Aunt Shannon brought her in here on purpose to make sure Vanessa won."

"Vanessa won fair and square," she said. "I saw it with my own eyes."

"She didn't break the rules," Chloe said in apologetic tones. "I watched her carefully."

"Sorry I left you behind," I said. "There's nothing remotely fair about what Aunt Shannon did, though. She was trying to create a scene."

"And you helped her do it," said Mum. "Your habit of making decisions without thinking them through has to stop, Robin."

"The chicken witnessed Anne's murder and might have vital information for the police," I pointed out. "Aunt Shannon has been tormenting her for the past day. Even if Vanessa herself didn't cheat, her mother is a potential suspect."

"That makes it all the more dangerous for you to get involved," Mum said. "My sister is not to be trifled with."

"I already snatched the sceptre from her grasp." If she wanted me dead, then I'd be more than happy to use the sceptre to apprehend her. "If you want me to hand Vanessa a trophy anyway, then I will, but I don't have to forget what she did."

"Then do as you like." Mum descended from the platform, leaving me alone with Chloe and Tansy.

"I should have gone after the chicken myself." Chloe hung her head.

"She was too fast for me to even use my magic on," I said. "I had to use the sceptre instead. I *am* sorry I left without you, though. I'm not used to having an assistant... or a bodyguard, either."

"I don't mind," she said. "Where do you want to go now? To your brother?"

Ramsey had taken over the questioning himself, but until I figured out how to undo the spell I'd cast on the chicken, I'd just be getting in his way. I had a few hours to myself before the trophy ceremony, but the odds of finding the killer in the interim were questionable.

"No," I said. "I think we should head back to my office."

Aunt Shannon would have to return home eventually, so I'd have no better chance to ambush her and demand to know what she'd done to scare the chicken so badly that she'd flown all the way across town.

Chloe and I walked in silence down the street towards home, and even Tansy seemed subdued. *I can't believe Vanessa won.* Mum might have been watching her every move, but I had a hard time believing she'd won the contest entirely on her own merit.

As I reached the coven's headquarters, Carmilla sat expectantly on the doorstep, waiting for me. "It might interest you to know the chicken has escaped."

"I'm aware of that," I said. "Didn't you try to stop her?"

"I'm too old to chase around your pets."

I scowled. "Was it Myrtle who chased her off?"

"Yes, it was." She yawned. "Rather mean of her, though I can't complain about how quiet the building is now she and the police have gone."

"Vanessa won the contest." A rush of anger hit me when I recalled Aunt Shannon's smirking face when she'd come downstairs to see Malcolm's body. I had a hard time believing she'd had no involvement. "Aunt Shannon isn't back yet?"

"No, she isn't," said Carmilla. "I gather she's pleased with herself."

"You might say that." Magic hummed in my fingertips in response to my growing fury, and the sound of birdsong echoed above as the local wildlife reacted. I clenched my fist. "Is Grandma back? Or is she still hiding?"

"Hiding?" Carmilla echoed. "She wouldn't like that tone of yours, you know."

"I'm used to that." The glow in my fingertips spread to the gem on the end of the sceptre too. Whoa. That was new. "My mother seems to think being Head Witch means taking a back seat."

"Of course she does," said Carmilla. "She expected to take the job herself. She's never been much of a fighter, despite her sharp tongue. Now, your grandmother, on the other hand… back in her prime, she used to take pride in turning her enemies into stone."

"She did?" I asked, disarmed. "I thought the title of Head Witch was supposed to be ceremonial."

"Obviously it is." The cat nudged open the door to the witches' headquarters. "Are you planning to come in?"

I didn't move. "I'd like to be the sort of Head Witch who fights her own battles. It'd have been nice if Grandma had told me that *was* an option."

"Talk to her yourself." Carmilla approached the door to my office. "Coming?"

"Wait, how did you get out? I thought the door was locked."

The cat raised her head. "I wouldn't be much of a Head Witch's familiar if I could be so easily trapped."

"*I'm* the Head Witch's familiar," Tansy announced. "And I hope nobody else got in."

"I can check," Chloe said quickly. "If that's okay with you, Head Witch."

"Go ahead." I walked over to the office door and unlocked it. "In fact, I have to do something else first. Can you check my desk and see if there's anything I need to attend to? I'll be back soon."

"Sure." Chloe went into the office, while I left the building with Tansy at my side.

Turning my back on the witches' headquarters, I strode down the road towards the house next to Mum's. Aunt Shannon wouldn't be back yet, but Vanessa would need to return home to get ready for the trophy ceremony at some point, and I was perfectly happy to wait outside her house for as long as necessary.

As it turned out, it took only ten minutes before Aunt Shannon and Vanessa approached the house. Aunt Shannon spotted me first. "What are you doing on my doorstep?"

"What do you want, Robin?" asked Vanessa. "You already said congratulations. Unless you want to do it properly this time."

Anger sparked, bringing light to my fingertips and the sceptre too. Aunt Shannon's gaze landed on the gem on the instrument's end, her eyes narrowing a fraction.

"It's your mother I wanted to talk to, Vanessa." I turned to my aunt. "Aunt Shannon, your familiar chased that chicken across town in order to disrupt the contest. Carmilla confirmed it was Myrtle who drove her out of the garden."

Aunt Shannon didn't even blink. "You trust that mangy old cat?"

"She's your late mother's familiar," I pointed out. "I'm inclined to believe her given that Myrtle has been tormenting the chicken—a familiar of a murder victim, I might add—for the past day."

"My familiar has good instincts," she said. "Right, precious?"

The magpie flew to land on her witch's shoulder and

cawed loudly. "For a Head Witch, you're rather dense, aren't you?"

"And just what is that supposed to mean?" I asked. "You expect me to ignore your tormenting an innocent familiar who belonged to a murder victim?"

"There is nothing innocent about that chicken," said Aunt Shannon. "She and her owner have been scheming together for years."

"How'd you figure that one out?"

"I did," said Vanessa. "I spoke to the other contenders on the first day, and they told me the chicken's owner was friends with Malcolm."

"Excuse me?" I looked between her and her mother while Tansy's tail began to wag. "Do you have proof of this? There's no documented connection between the pair of them at all."

"Obviously they didn't talk about it in public," said Vanessa. "But it's true. Malcolm sold potions to the entrants, while Anne made bets on who would emerge victorious. They raked in a fortune."

"Bets." That would explain what Malcolm would have to gain from rigging the contests, but how had Vanessa of all people managed to wring a confession from the other contenders? "Roxy always won, though. She never took him up on his offer."

"Doesn't matter," said Vanessa. "Enough people did that they had a nice little scheme going. You're welcome for the tip."

"There you have it," said Aunt Shannon. "Consider yourself lucky that my daughter was willing to share anything with you after the way you have treated her."

"I haven't treated her any differently from the other

contenders," I said. "Also, when I questioned her earlier, she claimed Malcolm never offered her any potions and acted as if she knew nothing at all."

"He didn't," she said. "But people talk. It wasn't hard to figure out what was going on."

"And—the murderer?" I shouldn't believe a word she said, yet her claims filled the gaps in my theories that even my brother had been struggling to figure out. "Anne and Malcolm both died. Are you saying it was a dissatisfied client who was responsible?"

Aunt Shannon laughed. "Leave the investigating to your brother, Head Witch. But I'll give you this information for free: that chicken and her owner came to murder you, and when Anne was foolish enough to get herself killed in the process, her familiar tried to finish the job."

Her words sent my mind into free fall. I gaped at her for a second, unable to believe she'd voiced my initial theory—that Anne had brought the cursed pens herself and accidentally died in the process.

"You're lying," Tansy said. "You can't know that."

"Ask the chicken yourself," added Vanessa. "Don't fall for her pathetic excuses this time."

"I don't think you're telling the full truth," I said. "What do you have to gain from helping me? You're waiting for me to drop dead so you can snatch the sceptre from my grip, aren't you?"

"Oh, I wouldn't presume to challenge the will of the sceptre," said Aunt Shannon. "You are undoubtedly its wielder... for now, anyway. Assuming you don't get yourself killed first."

She's lying. Or omitting the truth, anyway. Aunt Shannon

was trying to make me doubt myself so she could get one step closer to taking my place as Head Witch.

I gave her a glare. "What I do is none of your business, Aunt Shannon. I haven't forgotten Rowan."

I turned my back and left her and Vanessa behind, trying not to walk too fast as I retraced my steps to the coven's headquarters. Upon ducking into the lobby, I all but ran into the office.

"Chloe." I exhaled in relief when I found her sitting at her desk with Grandma's laptop open in front of her. "Is everything okay?"

"Sure," she said. "There's another letter on the desk for you to sign, by the way."

"Is there?" I picked up the container of pens, but Tansy moved in a blur, tackling it out of my hands. The pens scattered on the floor while Tansy landed on all fours on the desk.

"Someone else was in here." Her tail wagged, pointing over my shoulder. "Look."

I spun around, seeing the window was open a crack. "Carmilla? Did you see anyone come in?"

"No, but I was sleeping."

Chloe rose to her feet with an expression of complete horror on her face that matched my own sinking dread. The intruder had tried to get into my office again... and this time, they'd succeeded.

13

"Don't touch the pens," I told Chloe when she moved towards the fallen container. "We don't know which are cursed, if any of them are."

Someone had definitely been in here, but that didn't mean they'd tried to use the same method as beforehand. *How did they get in?* The window hadn't been forced, and it couldn't be opened from outside without an unlocking charm—which was impossible to cast without a wand.

Chloe wrung her hands. "I'm sorry. I should have seen."

"It's not your fault." I pulled out my phone and called my brother. "Hey, Ramsey. The intruder got into my office this time, and I'm pretty sure they left some cursed pens behind."

I hung up before he could do more than utter a sharp curse, which seemed utterly out of character for him. My nerves jangled as I paced around the desk, trying to figure out how the intruder had entered the office.

Carmilla perched on Chloe's desk, standing on her hind legs to look at the window. "It was opened from the inside."

"So the intruder got *out* through the window but not in?" I trod carefully around the spilled pens and peered over the cabinets. Given how cluttered the office was, there might well be a secret door back there that nobody had told me about. "Carmilla, are there any hidden entrances to the office behind the cabinets?"

"No," she said. "There are not."

So much for that theory.

"Well, they didn't walk through the wall." I made my careful way past the first row of cabinets, only for Chloe to grab my arm and drag me backwards.

"Don't touch anything! We don't know what else might be cursed."

"Not the cabinets." I obliged, though, since moving to the back of the office meant I was more likely than not to bring a mountain of paper crashing down on my head. "I'll let Ramsey search, then."

"Good idea." She stood stiffly beside the desk, looking at the pens as if they might leap up and bite her. "I can't believe someone did this."

"Really, this ought to be an argument in favour of me using computers instead of writing by hand." I did my best to keep my tone light despite my racing heart. "Grandma won't be able to complain if I tell her I narrowly avoided death by cursed pen."

Tansy snorted. "Do you think she'd accept that excuse?"

"Nah, probably not," I admitted. "I'd also like to know what she was doing during the break-in. A ghost who can travel through walls ought to be a better security guard than she has been."

Grandma hadn't shown her face in a while. Ghosts didn't need to sleep, so it was anyone's guess as to where she'd wandered off to, but her absence was the least of my worries. I stepped over the pens again as I crossed the room to the door, belatedly remembering the invisible ink I'd left outside. If the intruder hadn't entered that way, they wouldn't have had any traces on their hands, but this wasn't the first time someone had tried to get into the office.

A faint herbal smell caught in my nostrils. Frowning, I nudged the door open and followed the scent across the lobby to the area behind the front door. "Who put sage in here?"

"Certainly not me," said Carmilla.

"Sage repels ghosts." It couldn't have been an accident. The person who'd left the herbs out must have known Grandma's ghost was here. I'd thought only our coven was aware of her continued existence as a ghost but if Aunt Shannon was responsible, was *she* the intruder?

I crouched down to pick up the sage, only to spring to my feet when the door opened and Ramsey almost tripped over me. "Whoa. Robin, what are you doing down there?"

"Someone put sage on the floor," I said. "Not inside my office but outside. I assume they knew we had a resident ghost."

"I thought you said someone broke into your office."

"They did." Chloe beckoned him through the door. "Don't touch the pens. We don't know which might be cursed."

"Or how they got in," I added. "The window was opened from the inside. The door was untouched."

"I'll take care of the pens." He moved into the office, pulling on a pair of thick gloves. I, meanwhile, set about searching the rest of the lobby for any more sage that might have been "accidentally" left lying around. Once I'd tossed it outside, I returned to the office.

"Where's the chicken?" I asked Ramsey.

"Still at the police station," he replied. "And yes, she's still frozen. You did a thorough job."

"Good," I said. "Possibly. Aunt Shannon seems to think *she's* the murderer."

"I'm sorry, what?" He blinked at me. "You spoke to her? When?"

"A few minutes ago, I confronted her over her stunt with that chicken," I said. "She claimed that Vanessa still won fair and square, and that Anne and her chicken were the ones who originally wanted me dead."

"You don't believe her, do you?" said Tansy. "She was deflecting blame."

"She raised a few questions, though," I said. "Also, her theory explains how Anne showed up with that cursed pen in her pocket after everyone else had already surrendered any magical objects they possessed."

"You think she brought it herself?" Ramsey asked. "That's an interesting theory, but given that it came from Aunt Shannon, I'm not sure how much weight we ought to give it."

"I wouldn't believe her, but there's something not right about that chicken," I said. "Besides, who broke into my office? Everyone else was at the contest. All the *humans* were, anyway."

"You think the chicken broke into your office?" Tansy snickered with laughter. "Sorry, Robin, but can you imagine that ridiculous bird being stealthy enough to break in without leaving a complete mess everywhere?"

"I gave her free run of the building," I reminded her. "Which I shouldn't have done, considering she's still technically a suspect."

"I can't arrest a chicken," Ramsey said. "You're not joking... are you?"

"That's not all Vanessa and her mum told me," I said. "Vanessa claimed that Anne and Malcolm were working together to rig the contest, and they placed bets on the winners. That's what they had to gain from it."

Ramsey frowned. "How exactly did Vanessa find out?"

"She claims she talked to the other entrants," I said. "It's worth asking, at least."

"That will have to wait," he said. "I'm not inclined to believe her mother, certainly, but as long as that chicken remains under your spell, she can't be questioned."

Didn't I know it. I turned to Grandma's familiar. "Carmilla, do you think there might be some truth to that idea?"

"You think the chicken is the intruder?" She gave a yowl of laughter. "Even I couldn't sleep through her endless whining."

"Hilarious," I said. "I got rid of the sage. When will Grandma come back? Do you know?"

"I have absolutely no idea." She curled up on Chloe's desk again and closed her eyes.

Exasperated, I turned to Ramsey. "What do you suggest I do? Should I tell Aunt Shannon the police want to question her and see if she repeats the same story to you?"

"You can try, but I don't have time to deal with her," he said. "If anything else in this office is cursed, I need to remove it. Preferably before Mum comes back."

Right. Mum would want to hear an update, too, and I could only imagine her reaction when she found out I'd confronted Aunt Shannon *and* Vanessa alone. She might think Vanessa had won her victory fairly, but I couldn't see her readily accepting a chicken as a potential killer. In fairness, I wasn't so sure myself either.

"I'll leave you to it, then." I made my way out the back door to the garden, more to get out of the cramped space than anything else.

Tansy ran along the lawn which dominated the back garden. "I bet Tiffany's fuming over Persephone getting kicked out of the contest."

"She bought into Malcolm's scheme," I said. "I think Vanessa might have been telling the truth about him and Anne working together. Or at the very least about some of the contenders making money from placing bets. It's the logical way to explain Malcolm's methods."

"Except that implies most of the winners' victories have been invalid," said Tansy. "Unless Roxy was telling the truth, and she didn't cheat."

"Maybe she doesn't need to." I kept walking until I came to the hedge maze at the back of the coven's garden. "She and her familiar are close enough not to require a potion to communicate. Yet they lost to *Vanessa* of all people."

And now I had to ready myself to give her a trophy as if she deserved it.

As if sensing my thoughts, Tansy scampered up my side, climbing onto my shoulder to curl her tail around the back of my neck like a comforting scarf. "I believe you. I just don't trust a word Aunt Shannon says. Or Vanessa."

"Neither do I, but do you really trust that chicken either?" I asked. "Her 'helpless victim' screaming being an act wouldn't be the weirdest thing to happen in the last couple of days."

"I guess not." Tansy's tail tickled my ear. "I still wonder if the Henbanes might be up to their old tricks."

"I don't see anyone in their garden." I slowed my pace as we weaved our way through the maze and past the dragon-headed fountain in the centre. After Tessa's murder had been solved, Mum had removed the spell which prevented me from using the gate from the maze to the woodland path. Since I had zero desire to go back through the coven's headquarters and face my family, I unlocked the gate and made my way outside into the Wildwood.

The comforting sounds of wildlife and the hum of magic soothed my nerves despite my meandering thoughts. Maybe nobody at all in the contest was innocent, after all, but if none of them had told Ramsey of Anne's previous involvement with Malcolm, the quickest way to confirm or refute Vanessa's claims was to get that chicken to confess. Too bad she remained stuck under the spell I'd inadvertently put on her. I held up the sceptre, examining its gleaming edge. "I need to figure out how to undo that immobilising spell."

I wouldn't normally have expected to master a powerful magical object right away, but I'd had to dive headfirst into the job of Head Witch without any time to adjust, and it was no wonder I'd screwed a few things up along the way.

"If you're looking for someone to use for target practise, you're out of luck," said Tansy.

"I'm not that mean," I said. "What's the best spell to unfreeze that chicken, do you think?"

"Not a heating spell," she said firmly. "Unless you really fancy barbecued chicken wings."

"Tansy." I suppressed a laugh, unable to help myself. "I don't know what we'll do if it turns out she *is* guilty."

Arresting a chicken for attempted murder wasn't exactly how I'd expected the contest to end, but it was better than the culprit getting away. Not that she'd be going anywhere as long as she remained frozen. I lifted the sceptre and pointed it at the nearest object—a tree branch—before casting an immobilising spell.

"Did it work?" Tansy scaled the tree and jumped up and down on the branch. "Not sure. It feels pretty sturdy, though."

"I should have picked something more mobile to practise on." I turned around and then jumped a foot in the air when I saw Harvey of all people watching me through the trees. "I didn't see you there."

"Sorry I startled you." He walked over to join me. "I don't think I've seen the sceptre up close before."

"I'm not having much luck with it." I lowered the sceptre, fighting the urge to unburden myself and tell him everything. He didn't want me sobbing on him about my failings, and besides, I was supposed to be catching a killer.

"The sceptre chose you," he said. "Didn't it? I admit I'm not an expert on the subject."

"It chose me, but I'm pretty sure it has a mind of its own." I definitely wasn't the best witch for the job by anyone's standards, and I suspected that if it hadn't been me who'd intercepted Grandma's killer, it would have chosen Mum instead. "Wish I'd had a trial run first."

Harvey studied my face. "Are you okay?"

"I turned a chicken into a statue earlier, and now I can't figure out how to undo it." So much for not running my mouth off. I sat down on a raised tree root and rested my head on my knees. "Also, I've been barred from my own office because an intruder got inside, and apparently the Head Witch isn't allowed to fight her own battles."

"An intruder?" His brows rose in alarm. "Are you in danger?"

"The Head Witch is never *not* in danger." Upon seeing the genuine concern on his face, I added, "It's not the intruder who's bothering me, it's the fact that I'm supposed to let everyone else deal with the hands-on work while I sit behind the scenes, signing letters when I'm not handing out trophies for inane competitions. I don't know how Grandma handled it." If Carmilla was to be believed, she'd taken matters into her own hands more than once, yet nobody seemed inclined to let me do the same without a fuss.

"Is your family still giving you trouble?" he asked. "I'm sure they have a lot to adjust to, but you're the Head Witch. You outrank them. Technically speaking."

"He's right," said Tansy. "Your mother appointed you an assistant without asking permission first, didn't she?

And she elbowed you out of the investigation when you have every right to be involved."

"I don't know what your familiar is saying, but I'm guessing she agrees with me," Harvey said. "I imagine your mother is adjusting to sharing responsibilities with another person, but that's no reason to disrespect you."

"True, but I *did* screw up with the chicken." Harvey's confused expression prompted me to add, "The chicken might be a murder suspect, but I turned her into a statue before we could get her to confess. It's been a really weird week."

"Sounds that way," he said. "Is that why you're practising with the sceptre?"

"Yeah… I haven't even had time to learn how to use it properly yet," I admitted. "It's like a supercharged wand that glows occasionally. Mum insists it's more of a ceremonial item than a magical weapon, but I'm starting to wish I'd been born in the days when being Head Witch meant fighting duels."

"I'm far from an expert in coven history, but isn't that why they used to have to appoint a new Head Witch so frequently?" he asked. "They kept getting killed or maimed?"

"True." I might not have remembered everything from my lessons, but I knew that a fair few of the coven's customs had come about to keep the Head Witch from a premature death. "Grandma was ninety-two, though, so it's understandable that she'd have wanted to take a back seat."

"Her familiar spends all her time sleeping." Tansy scampered around my feet. "Who says either of us has to follow in the last Head Witch's footsteps?"

Everyone. Or so it felt like, anyway. "I thought I could put up with the meetings... even the paperwork. But I don't think I can deal with being shut away when someone wants me dead."

"Someone wants you dead?" Alarm flitted across Harvey's face. "They're after you right now?"

"Yes, and Ramsey has all but shoved me out of the investigation," I said. "Mum keeps lecturing me about not breaking with tradition. Carmilla hinted my grandmother used to be more of a hands-on Head Witch, but that was a long time ago."

"Isn't every Head Witch different?" he asked. "Not that I'm advising you to go chasing a potential killer alone, but your family should give you space to decide how you want to run things."

"I thought I'd started to get through to them, but I guess not." I rose to my feet. "I should go, anyway. I'm losing track of time in here, and I have to go and announce my cousin as the contest's winner soon."

"She won?" he asked.

"Vanessa did, yes," I said. "You can come to the ceremony if you'd like to see me make a public fool of myself."

"I'm sure you won't," he said. "Focus on what's important to you, not them. I don't know if that helps, but it's what I try to do when I'm having a dispute with my team. Stick to your guns."

"That does help," I said. "I hope we do get to have our date at some point this century."

He laughed. "It's early days, like I said. I'll see you soon."

"I'll let you know when I'm free."

I watched him walk away down the path, debating for

a moment whether it was worth returning to my office. The intruder would be long gone by now, and knowing Ramsey, he'd have cordoned the place off while he searched for any more curses hidden inside.

I found myself wandering farther down the woodland trail, turning the clues over in my mind. The intruder couldn't have been from among the contenders. As far as I was aware, none of them had been missing from the arena except the ones who were already dead or under questioning by the police. That alone pointed to Aunt Shannon's involvement, but it didn't explain why she'd sent the chicken fleeing the garden too. Of course, there was an easy way to find out if she'd tried to get into my office... look for signs of that glowing ink on her hands.

"Should we turn off the lights at the trophy ceremony to see who lights up?" asked Tansy when I mentioned this aloud. "Might work."

"That'd expose the intruder... if they're in the room." Yet there were other clues which remained unexplained. Anne and Malcolm and their scheming, which went back years. The Henbanes and whether Persephone had done worse than cheat...

I came to a halt. Somehow, my steps had brought me to the cottage where Dad lived with his wife, Jessica, and her two werewolf kids. They'd both said I could drop by any time, but that had been days ago, before I'd been Head Witch. I wasn't yet sure if the same applied now that I had a sceptre in my hand and a target on my back.

Before I could retreat into the woods, the door opened, and Dad came out. "Robin! I wondered what you'd been up to."

"You haven't heard?" I approached the cottage, taking

in the welcome sight of my ordinary father, whose life was a world away from mine. Short and round, he had a growing bald patch amid his grey hair, but his smile was as infectious as it'd been when I was a kid.

When Jessica came into view behind him, her smile was more forced, less certain. "Oh… it's you, Head Witch."

"You can still call me Robin," I said to the blond werewolf. "Sorry. I was just walking in the woods. I don't want to intrude."

"I did say you could drop by anytime," Dad said. "Didn't you have some kind of big ceremony this evening?"

"Yeah… the trophy ceremony for the Familiar Contest, but that doesn't start for a while."

The sound of delighted squealing came from behind the house.

"The boys are playing in the back garden," said Jessica.

"Perks of living near the forest," I said. "Must be fun."

"Come and look." Dad beckoned me around the side of the cottage through a patch of trees, from which I could see two fluffy werewolves tumbling around in the grass. Adorable.

"Somehow they make *more* mess when they're in the form of wolves," Jessica said. "Despite being smaller. Pity shifters don't qualify to enter a contest like that one, because I think they'd win."

"I bet." I watched them tumbling over one another, thoughts clinking against each other in my mind. "I'm guessing you heard Vanessa won the contest, Dad?"

He grimaced. "Her? Really?"

"Yeah, and I can't accuse her of cheating because I was chasing a runaway chicken at the time."

"Eventful week, then?"

"You might say that." I'd have to tell him everything later, but judging by the way the sun had begun to sink behind the treetops, I had less than an hour to get ready for the ceremony. "Never a dull moment when you're Head Witch."

"If it makes you feel any better, I doubt I could deal with the pressure," he said. "You're doing great."

"It doesn't feel that way," I admitted. "I need to decide what kind of Head Witch I'm going to be, I think."

"Don't let anyone rush you," said Dad. "You can figure it out in your own time."

He had his own share of experience with Mum's controlling nature, so he knew exactly what I was dealing with. "I'll try."

Dad had met Jessica several years after he and Mum had split up, and while the coven and the press had made no secret of their disdain for him marrying a werewolf, he seemed far happier here than he'd been while married to Mum. I could see the appeal of living out of the spotlight, and while that kind of life wasn't in the cards for me, I was glad his door was open for me to run to when the job of Head Witch grew too overwhelming."

"You should get to that ceremony of yours," he said. "See you soon?"

"Sure. I'll try to drop by later this week."

I turned my back on the cottage and left via the woodland path, feeling considerably more upbeat despite the looming prospect of handing Vanessa a trophy. Tansy ran around the forest while I walked back, chasing birds to her heart's content. Then she let out a shriek that had me running to her side.

"Tansy!" I came to a halt where she'd paused, halfway down a tree, sniffing at a small hole at the base of the trunk. "What is it?"

"I nearly *trod* on it."

I peered into the hole, and my heart lurched. Several pens lay inside, barely concealed underneath a pile of grass cuttings.

"That's where the killer hid their weapons." The hole was small enough that a person would have trouble getting inside... but a small animal wouldn't. Like the chicken, for instance.

I grabbed my phone. "Let's tell Ramsey."

14

Fifteen minutes later, I was at the police station again. I'd all but resigned myself to being late for the trophy ceremony by this point, but with the police searching the forest and the coven in an uproar, it wouldn't have surprised me if it ended up being postponed anyway.

Ramsey walked out of one of the offices. "Those pens are secured, but the killer might have had more than one hiding place in the forest."

"I know," I said. "They were well hidden. I'd never have found them if Tansy hadn't been in the tree at the time."

"Tricky." Tansy looked over my shoulder at Ramsey's office. "Are Minty and Jarvis still in there?"

"Yes, and I still haven't managed to undo that spell of yours yet," Ramsey said. "Are you sure Minty has information?"

"Yes," I said. "If she didn't break into my office, then she still worked with Anne when she was helping

Malcolm run his cheating scheme. I'm certain she has more to tell us."

"If Vanessa told the truth." He approached his office and opened the door, revealing the chicken sitting on the desk in a pile of frozen feathers. "Can you undo the spell?"

"I don't know. Maybe I should cast a different one instead." If my immobilising spell had stopped her for hours at a time, then maybe some kind of motion spell would be needed to undo it. "What's the opposite to an immobilising spell?"

"Didn't you pay any attention in lessons?"

I frowned at him. "Sorry if I didn't anticipate having to unfreeze a potential murder suspect who also happens to be a chicken. Would a motion spell do?"

"Yes, it would." He walked over to the desk. "Are you sure about this?"

"Nope, but that's a running theme this week." I nodded to him. "Hold her in case she tries to run."

Then I pointed the sceptre at her, giving it a wave. A jet of light shot from the end, colliding with the chicken. At once, Ramsey's grip broke as the chicken leapt into the air, bouncing off the walls like a Ping-Pong ball and upending Ramsey's carefully arranged desk. Jarvis ran from underneath with a yowl of displeasure, and when I caught him, his claws sank into my wrist.

"Ow." I lost my grip on the cat, but Ramsey wasn't having much luck with the chicken either. She continued to zip around the office, and it wasn't until she crashed headlong into a cabinet that she came to a halt.

"I think it wore off," Tansy remarked from where she'd perched on the windowsill.

"You think?" I rubbed my sore wrist and approached the dazed-looking chicken. "Sorry about that, Minty."

"You tried to kill me!" shrieked the chicken. "Like Anne!"

"We're not the ones who killed her." She might well have accidentally touched the pen herself while trying to kill *me*, but the only way to find out was to push ahead with a proper interrogation. "I need to ask you some questions. Why were you at the arena?"

"That magpie chased me." She sobbed. "She wouldn't leave me alone."

"Did you talk to the woman too?" I asked. "Her owner?"

"She insulted my witch," she said. "She accused me of horrible things."

"Like what?" I asked. "Did she imply that Anne brought those cursed pens to town herself?"

She made a whimpering noise. "Slander."

"It isn't true?" Ramsey stepped in behind me. "We need to know who broke into Robin's office. The break-in occurred around the same time as you were chased out of the building, by my estimate."

"Not me, not me!" She began flapping her wings in agitation again.

"Did you see anything, then?" I asked. "At the office?"

"No." The sheer number of feathers she'd left from her panicked flight made it unlikely that I wouldn't have found any traces of her in my office, but I couldn't yet rule out the possibility that she'd been involved.

I drew in a breath. "Is it true that Anne worked with Malcolm, helping him cheat by offering free potions to the contenders and placing bets on who she thought would win?"

She gave a startled squawk. "What?"

A hissing noise came from near the door, where Jarvis had found his path out of the office blocked by Tansy.

"Where do you think you're going?" she asked.

"Is it true?" I addressed the cat instead. "Did the two of them work together? Anne and Malcolm, rigging the contest and placing bets on the winners?"

"I will not speak ill of the dead," said Jarvis.

"That means it's true." I turned to Ramsey. "Aunt Shannon and Vanessa got some of it right after all, but does that make Anne and Malcolm conspirators in murder as well?"

Minty made an indistinct squeaking noise. "No, no! She never harmed anyone!"

"If you want to find out who killed her, then I need you to tell me what you know." I kept my gaze on Minty, who seemed a little steadier now that the effects of the spell had worn off. "Did you see her killer?"

"Maybe—I don't know."

"Who?" Ramsey asked. "What does that mean? You saw the person who gave her the pen?"

"I think so." The chicken whimpered again. "Anne— she ran into someone when we first arrived in town. I didn't hear what he said to her, but she looked scared, and I think *he* gave her that pen!"

"Who was he, though?" I asked. "One of the contenders?"

"No. I don't know." She began to rock back and forth on the desk.

Ramsey approached her. "What did he look like? Tell me everything you saw."

She gasped. "He had blond hair, and he was wearing these odd clothes that were far too big for him. If he killed her... you have to find him, Head Witch."

"He's not a contender," I murmured. "Then who?"

"Whoever it is, we'll have to find him later," Ramsey said. "The ceremony starts in five minutes."

"You think that's my priority? Really?"

"The contenders will all be there," he said. "So will half the town. I can ask my team to keep an eye out for trouble, but you need to attend the ceremony yourself."

I swallowed my annoyance, recalling my earlier plan to expose the intruder. "Tansy, do you think you can turn the lights off in the town hall without anyone seeing you?"

"It'd be my pleasure."

"What on earth are you talking about?" asked Ramsey.

"The mysterious person who gave Anne the pen might not be there, but if they had an accomplice who broke into my office, the glow-in-the-dark ink will give them away pretty quickly."

I beckoned to Tansy to follow me out of his office, ignoring his exasperated sigh. Mum wouldn't approve of my plan either, but she'd be angrier that I'd showed up for the trophy ceremony dressed in the same clothes I'd worn to the contest earlier. Ah, well. If I was going to end up chasing a killer, there was no sense in dressing my best.

I neared the town hall, doing my best to push down my apprehension. There was a good chance the killer would be waiting somewhere among the crowd, and given the number of pens we'd found in the forest, they hadn't wanted to leave anything to chance. That suggested to me that they wouldn't leave town until I was dead or they were locked up for their crimes.

Chloe met me in the entryway. "Head Witch! I brought you a dress."

"You brought me what?" I asked, nonplussed.

She handed me a bundle of fabric. "Quick, go and change. You still have time."

"I—thank you." I tucked the dress under my arm. "You might have saved me a lecture."

She gave me a shy smile. "You have enough to worry about without Lady Wildwood disapproving of your choice in clothes."

I might not have asked for an assistant, but she'd gone above and beyond what I might have expected, and I owed her one for this. I took the dress into the ladies' toilets to change before approaching the twin oak doors leading into the main hall.

When I entered, I found the hall had been newly decorated with bright banners and clusters of balloons. A buffet table stood on one side of the hall, and a band played on the stage at the front. This was all Mum's work, I thought with a pang of guilt. She might have spoken harshly to me, but considering she'd spent weeks putting together the contest only for the killer to attempt to derail everything, the least I could do was help bring the event to a satisfying end.

Even if it did mean being nice to Vanessa.

I caught Mum's eye and approached her. "This looks nice."

"Thank you for your approval, Head Witch." The slightest edge to her words squashed the guilt I'd felt at ruining her day. "We need to have a talk later."

"Yes, we do." No doubt she wanted to give me a long lecture, but that could wait until after I'd thwarted the killer. "Before that, though, I have a murderer to expose."

Mum's expression stilled. "You know who did it?"

"I know how to expose their accomplices," I said. "Aunt Shannon won't be thrilled if I deprive Vanessa of her glory, but this ceremony is the last time all the contenders will be in the same room."

"I will handle my sister," she said to my surprise. "As for exposing the killer, I would appreciate it if you gave me more information."

"I want to be honest with everyone to the best of my ability," I said. "They won't expect me to outright state that there's a killer after me."

If that didn't coax the killer out of hiding, then exposing the accomplice was the next best thing.

Her eyes clouded with what might have been concern. "That plan might backfire on you, Robin."

"It's a gamble," I acknowledged, "but the killer must know we're getting close. They've spent all this time sneaking around in the shadows, and I think it's past time we put the spotlight on them."

"It's your choice," she said, "but remember that all eyes are on you."

"Hard to forget." In a way, being the Head Witch's granddaughter had prepared me for taking on the position, if not in the way most people might have expected.

I can handle this. I have to.

Sceptre in hand, I waited for the contenders to enter the hall. They arrived in groups, dressed in their finest, admiring the band and the decorations. All the contenders, winners and losers, were invited to the ceremony… and if the killer was among them, we'd expose them for everyone to see.

"This time, we'll get them," I muttered.

"Yes, we will," Tansy said. "If you don't keep talking to yourself when everyone can hear you, that is."

"I'm not holding a microphone yet," I pointed out. "When I give you the signal, that's your cue to turn out the lights."

"I can't wait."

Neither could I. Waiting wasn't my style, but I stood as patiently as I could muster until the hall was full and Vanessa stood expectantly in front of the stage where I would present her with her trophy. She must have used a quick spell to curl her blond hair and had put on a pretty red dress. Yet all eyes were on me instead when I held up the sceptre and climbed onto the stage.

"Welcome," I said to the crowd. "And congratulations again to the finalists of the Familiar Contest. All three of those who made it to the final round will be getting a prize tonight."

Cheering and applause ensued, petering out when I raised the sceptre again. "Before I give the awards out, however, I want to offer my apologies for disappearing during the final round of the contest."

A scattering of laughter rose from some of the people who'd seen me chasing the chicken, but Vanessa merely looked annoyed at having her big moment delayed.

"The truth is, I was targeted by an assassination attempt," I went on. "Someone used the contest as an opportunity to try to kill the Head Witch."

Shocked whispers rose among the crowd.

"What's more…" I raised my voice a little. "I believe the person responsible is within this very room."

More gasps echoed throughout the hall, at which point I caught sight of Tansy's bright-red tail and gave the slightest nod.

A moment later, the lights went out, plunging the entire hall into darkness. The gasps among the crowd rose in volume, while a bright glow drew my gaze downward. Oops. I'd accidentally got some of the ink on my own hands—but another equally bright glow came from within the audience. A small patch of brightness against the dark.

Purple light ignited the sceptre, signalling to Tansy. An instant later, the lights came back on, but I kept my attention trained on the place I'd seen the glow coming from. Nolan… or rather, the rat sitting at his feet. The instant the rat saw me looking, he bolted, his small, furry form streaking through the crowd.

"Someone catch that rat!" I shouted.

Pandemonium broke out as humans and familiars looked around for the source of the ruckus, but the rat moved far too fast for me to track. By the time I caught up to Tansy near the door, she said, "He got outside!"

I spun around to look for his owner, seeing that Nolan had been surrounded, packed in by the crowd. "Don't let him get away!"

"Robin." Ramsey entered the hall, breathless. "What —?"

"Nolan's rat got away," I said. "Don't let him escape too."

"His *rat?*"

"He had glow-in-the-dark ink all over his little feet,

Ramsey," I said. "Nolan is in there, but I bet he'll try to join him."

"Right." Ramsey moved into the hall, raising his voice. "Step aside, everyone. Let me through."

I hovered near the door, ready to use the sceptre if necessary, but Ramsey had Nolan secured in handcuffs impressively fast and across the hall just as quickly. Mum was trying to restore order, but everyone seemed to have forgotten the contest entirely. It wasn't until I climbed onto the stage and held up the large silver trophy that eyes began to turn in my direction again.

I reached out to Mum for the microphone. "My apologies for the interruption. It's now time for me to present the winners with their prizes. Congratulations to the first-place winner of the Familiar Contest, Vanessa Wildwood."

Hardly anyone clapped. They were too busy trying to see what was happening outside the door or whispering to one another. Meanwhile, Vanessa snatched the trophy from my hands in mute anger and stood rigidly on the stage while I offered the second- and third-place winners their own prizes. Once Roxy and Patrick had their trophies in hand, I climbed off the stage and handed the microphone back to Mum. "Can you keep everyone in here while I find our missing rat?"

"Isn't your brother looking for him?" she asked. "There are a lot of hiding places for a familiar."

"He wants me dead," I said. "I bet I can draw him out of hiding."

Mum worked her jaw, as if chewing on the words she wanted to say. In the end, all she said was, "Be careful."

"I'll do my best."

Aunt Shannon barred my way when I tried to leave the hall. "Where are you going this time?"

"To find the killer," I said. "It's not becoming of a Head Witch to allow others to take the hit for me."

"You made a fool of my daughter."

"I handed her the trophy, didn't I?" I pointed out. "If she wants to lend her help to find our missing contender, then it'd be welcome."

"What contender?" Aunt Shannon's face was bright red, but she couldn't dispute the fact that I'd done my job. "You can't expect us to believe the murderer was a mere rodent."

"The intruder certainly was," I said. "We'll see what happens when I catch him."

I sidestepped her and left the hall, going in search of my would-be killer.

15

Outside the town hall, I found Ramsey hurrying back from the police station.

"Where's the rat?" I asked.

"Lost sight of him," he replied. "Nolan is in custody, but he's not talking."

"Maybe he'll talk to me." I hadn't a hope of spotting a rat in the near darkness, but I found it hard to believe Nolan hadn't known what his familiar was up to. "He might know where his rat ran off to."

Ramsey glanced over his shoulder at me. "I shouldn't, but—fine. Come with me."

Fine minutes later, Ramsey and I sat on one side of a table in one of the police station's interrogation rooms, while Nolan sat opposite us, his hands in cuffs and a resigned expression on his face. "What do you want, Head Witch?"

"That's not very polite," I said. "Why did you enter the contest? Tell me the truth."

Nolan said nothing in response.

"You can stay quiet if you like," Ramsey said, "but unless you speak in your own defence, we can only assume you're as guilty of murder as your familiar is."

He blanched. "Murder? No."

"Then tell me the truth," I said. "Were you aware that prior to their deaths, Malcolm and Anne were running a scheme to make money from these contests by rigging the results and helping the contenders cheat?"

His face flushed. "Yes, but I didn't kill them."

"I find it hard to believe your rat carried those pens to town single-handedly," I said. "Why *did* you enter the contest?"

"To expose their cheating," he said. "I didn't expect them to die."

"And why was your familiar in my office?" It didn't take a genius to figure out that he'd sneaked into the office more than once, but had Nolan told him to do it? If not, who *was* the rat?

Nolan didn't answer, but Ramsey rose to his feet and beckoned me to follow him out of the room.

I waited for a moment before joining him. "If his rat is the one who engineered this, can you lock up a familiar but not his owner?"

Ramsey shook his head. "I'll have to look up the rules on familiars. They certainly have a will of their own."

"Yes, we do," said Tansy. "But he's no familiar."

A shiver ran over my arms, though I'd suspected the same deep down.

Ramsey simply looked bewildered. "If he's not a familiar, what is he, then?"

"A rat *shifter*." I looked over at Nolan, not bothering to lower my voice, and he averted his gaze. "I should have known something was wrong with him when he wouldn't talk to me. Shifters don't count as animals, so my ability doesn't work on them."

Ramsey ducked back into the room. "Did you know?"

Nolan kept his attention on the table. "Know what?"

I returned to my seat. "That your familiar was a shifter in disguise. You must have."

"I did." He spoke haltingly. "I don't have a familiar of my own, so it was the only way I could enter the contest. He volunteered to help me for a cut of the prize money if we won."

"So you think cheating is okay if you have the right intentions?" That was beside the point, though. "I'm guessing he tried to break into my office several times as a human before deciding to sneak in as a rat instead."

No doubt when we searched behind those cabinets, we'd find a rat-shaped hole in the wall. The sage might have been Aunt Shannon's doing, but it was the rat who'd smuggled the lethal pens into my office.

"I'll conduct another search of your office," said Ramsey as if he'd sensed my thoughts. "The rat has never been seen as a human?"

"I bet it was him who ran into Anne before the contest started," I said. "He slipped the pen into her pocket during their altercation. She and Minty didn't recognise him as a contender because he wasn't one, not really."

"Is that true?" Ramsey asked Nolan. "Did you know?"

"I didn't know the pens would kill the person who touched them," he said. "That's the truth."

"You can't accidentally commission someone to cast an illegal curse," I said. "Where'd you get them from? Was that the rat too?"

If his rat was guilty of both crimes, it didn't surprise me that he'd bolted as soon as he'd been caught, but he wouldn't shift back into human form until he found a safe place to hide. Most shifters couldn't use magic, so I didn't need to fear him sneaking up on me when I had the sceptre... unless he had more of those pens, of course. But he couldn't touch them with his bare hands without succumbing to the curse himself.

"We need to find him," Ramsey said in a low voice. "If he's a rat, he doesn't even have any clothes on his back, let alone a wand."

"Precisely my thinking," I said. "In fact, Minty said the guy Anne ran into when she arrived in town was wearing clothes that looked like they didn't fit. I bet he borrowed or stole them from someone when he landed."

Someone hammered on the door. "Ramsey, can you come out here a second?"

"Sure." He opened the door to reveal several officers gathering outside. "What's going on?"

"That cat *and* chicken both tried to escape your office at the same time," said one of the officers. "Scratched up my ankle in the process too."

"Oh no." I spun around, seeing Tansy darting out of sight through the automatic doors. "Tansy!"

I heard Ramsey trying to explain, but I was more focused on catching up to my own familiar than explaining that the rat they were looking for wasn't a familiar at all. Luckily, Tansy's bright tail was easy to spot even in the darkness.

The chicken and the cat, though, had vanished. "Did you see where they went?"

"No," said Tansy. "I bet I know who they're looking for, though. Their owners' murderer."

"Yeah." The streets were dark by now despite the lights shining in the windows of the nearby pubs and houses. "I can cast a light spell."

"I'd rather not be blinded, thanks."

"Ha ha." I held up the sceptre's glowing purple gem to use as a torch, and a thud sounded from nearby.

I followed the noise to the dark exterior of Were's My Coffee?, where Carmilla bounded out of the shadows, pinning a rat's tail under her paw. The glow around his paws gave him away as the murderer. *There he is.*

"Don't eat that rat," I told her. "He's human."

"Is that why he smells so foul?" She wrinkled her nose.

"Yes," I said. "I wonder if he'll shift into a human when you dig your claws in."

The rat wriggled free of her grip, but Tansy pounced on him first. She was around the same size as he was, but she did a valiant job of holding him down for a few seconds before the rat broke free in a wild lunge, streaking across the street.

Jarvis emerged from the darkness and pounced. There came a crash, a squeak, and then a naked man was lying on the side of the road under Jarvis's claws. For some reason, I hadn't factored the clothing loss into the scenario of confronting my would-be killer. *This is awkward.*

"I think I preferred you as a rat," I told the strange blond man. "What's your real name?"

"None of your business." He shifted back into a rat and tried to sprint off, but Carmilla pinned him once again, her teeth bared.

Once again, he shifted into the form of a blond male human with a defeated look on his face. "I'll come quietly."

"Why pens?" I didn't know why *that* was the first question to come out of my mouth, but this had to be the weirdest interrogation I'd ever been involved in. "Why do you want me dead?"

For the third time, he shifted into a rat and ran for his life, dodging the claws and paws that tried to pin him down. This time, I waved the sceptre and cast a freeze-frame spell, causing him to skid to a dead stop.

After striding over to him, I picked the rat up by the tail and carried him back to the police station. The officers all gawked at me when I entered via the automatic doors.

Ramsey hurried to my side. "Is that him?"

"I'd put him in a cell before I undo the spell I used on him," I said. "I want to know if he's acting alone."

"You think he isn't?" asked Ramsey.

"He seems to have a grudge against me, but I've never seen him in my life," I said. "He and Nolan came here to disrupt the cheating scam, allegedly, but there's got to be another scheme at work."

"I'll put him in the holding cells." Ramsey took the rat by the tail, while Minty and Jarvis looked on in satisfaction from the doorway.

I followed Ramsey through to a short corridor that led to the holding cells. Several people sat in small cells behind bars... including Persephone Henbane.

She shot me a hurt look. "Do you always treat your guests so badly? You denied me a trophy, shut me in a cage, and forgot about me."

"I didn't forget." The final piece of the puzzle slid into place. "Was it all Tiffany's doing, or did you have a hand in their scheme?"

She blinked at me. "I'm sorry, what?"

"You heard me," I said. "Nolan's rat familiar was working with more than one person at once. Nolan asked him to sneak into the contest to expose the cheating scams, but someone else wanted him to help assassinate the Head Witch without leaving a trail leading back to the person who hired him."

Persephone was silent for a heartbeat. "You're mad."

"You didn't say I was wrong."

Who else among the contenders had such a grudge against my family that they'd be willing to go to such lengths to have me killed? The contenders didn't know me, but Persephone did.

Ramsey stepped up to her cell. "Two people are dead. If you are in any way involved, then I'd advise you to make a confession."

"You've clearly decided I'm guilty." She raised her head, her eyes bright with defiance. "The Head Witch is a fraud, and it's about time the Wildwood witches were ousted from the power they've held over the rest of us for so many years."

"So you decided to target me because you think I'm a weak link?" I moved closer to the cell. "You're wrong. And you'll stay behind bars for a long time for what you did."

I turned my back on her and instead moved to the cell in which Ramsey had put the rat.

"Are you going to turn him back?" he asked.

"You know what? I think I'll leave him like that for a

while." I walked past Nolan, also ensconced in one of the holding cells. "Him too."

"I'll have to properly interrogate them tomorrow," said Ramsey. "And then there's the matter of what to do with Minty and Jarvis too."

"Good point," I said. "Their owners weren't exactly morally scrupulous, but a familiar losing their witch or wizard is punishment enough. We should let them go."

"The Henbanes." Ramsey spoke in a low voice which nevertheless reverberated with uncharacteristic anger. "Of course it was them. Why didn't I see it before?"

"They took care to cover their tracks," I reminded him. "They didn't even seem to be trying all that hard to kill me."

"Nevertheless." He blew out a breath. "We still haven't tracked down the creator of those cursed pens either."

"I know," I said. "Also, we'll need to hunt down any rat-shaped holes behind all those cabinets in my office. Preferably before Grandma's ghost comes back."

"You're going back now?"

"No," I said. "I think I should go back to the ceremony. For Mum's sake."

I left the police station with Tansy and made my way through the dark street towards the town hall. In the entryway, though, I found Harvey Walton hovering outside the oak doors.

"What are you doing here?" I asked.

"Looking for you," he said. "I heard something about a rat... and a murderer."

"The murderer is behind bars," I said. "And my brother is going to take care of the rest while I tell my mother. You weren't coming to the trophy ceremony, were you?"

"I don't have anything else to do tonight," he said. "I like the dress, by the way."

A flush crept up my neck. "It's not exactly designed for chasing killers around, but it does the job."

I felt like I was walking through a dream as Harvey and I entered the main hall and joined the crowd celebrating Vanessa's victory... or rather, celebrating the murderer's arrest, even if they didn't know all the details yet. Even Mum. That would be a fun conversation, but Harvey's presence at my side indicated he had no intention of leaving me to face her alone.

This wasn't the first date I'd expected, but it was the next best thing.

16

I returned to my office the following morning, feeling surprisingly alert considering how late I'd stayed up the previous night. First at the trophy ceremony, then helping Mum clean up the aftermath and checking in with my brother. It'd been a fun evening considering how badly it'd started, and the fact that Vanessa had left the party early in a huff was just the icing on the cake.

To top it all off, I had my office back, and I started my day by casting a barrier spell over the back wall until Ramsey was able to come over and help me hunt down any gaps so that no more small animals managed to sneak in. Or shifters, as the case may be. A shimmering semi-transparent shield now covered the entirety of the cabinets stacked against the back wall.

"That ought to do it." I regarded my work with satisfaction and lowered the sceptre. "If I have to wait until the weekend for Ramsey to help me move all those cabinets, then at least I'm less likely to get ambushed by any more intruders."

"It should stop those papers from falling on your head too," Tansy remarked.

"Always a bonus," I said. "Now I have two days of work to catch up on."

Grandma wouldn't be thrilled, but I still hadn't seen any signs of her since before I'd disposed of the sage I'd found behind the front door. I was inclined to blame Aunt Shannon for that one, but I was also pretty sure the rat wouldn't have been able to break in if Grandma's ghost had been around. The bonus to her absence was that she wasn't around to berate me for opening the laptop instead of picking up a pen and paper. Not that there were many pens in sight after Ramsey had insisted on checking every single one of them for lethal curses.

Chloe helped me navigate my way through the new accounts she'd created for me. "Everything's there, so you can arrange the desktop to your liking. I still don't have the passwords for the former Head Witch's account, though."

"No worries," I said. "I'll write mine down on paper so that future Head Witches don't have the same issue."

I opened the calendar app to find that Chloe had already filled in all the meetings on my schedule for the next few weeks. Of which there were a lot.

"You have a meeting this afternoon," Tansy read over my shoulder. "What are you doing until then?"

"Removing *that*, I hope." Grandma's ghost appeared in front of the desk, pointing at the shielding spell I'd put over the cabinets.

I jumped out of my seat. "There you are."

"Well observed," she said. "What *did* you do to my cabinets?"

"A shielding spell," I said. "There's a hole in the wall back there which allowed an intruder to sneak in, so I took precautions until I can remove the cabinets and check."

"You'll do no such thing," she said. "I have everything where I want it."

Now I remembered why I'd been so relieved when she'd first disappeared. "Grandma, someone broke in here and tried to kill me with a cursed pen yesterday."

"So that's where all the pens have disappeared to."

"You don't need pens. You're a ghost."

"Nobody has any respect for me anymore, do they?" She sniffed. "First you left sage outside the door and now this."

"I didn't leave that sage out, Grandma," I said. "I think it was Aunt Shannon, but it might as easily have been the person who wanted me dead. You know, they almost succeeded precisely because there could be a wild manticore hidden at the back of those cabinets and I'd have no idea."

"I am fairly sure you'd smell a wild manticore, Robin."

"Hilarious." I shook my head. "You're welcome to stay in here, but the office is mine, and I need to be able to keep it secure against further intruders. You haven't even asked *who* wanted me dead."

"I imagine you were about to tell me," she said.

"Persephone Henbane."

"That one?" She snorted with laughter, startling Chloe and waking Carmilla from her nap. "I hardly think she's a mastermind."

"Well, Tiffany hasn't confessed to anything," I said. "Or even come to her niece's defence. It was quite the scheme, though. She had a local rat shifter acquire several cursed pens and then smuggle them into the Familiar Contest by hiding among the contenders' familiars."

"I could have told you myself that the Henbane witches would be first in line to see you lose your title," she said. "I *did* tell you, in fact."

"You didn't say they were planning to assassinate me," I said. "Anyway, Aunt Shannon was acting suspiciously too. I'm pretty sure she's the one who left sage out there."

"I'd expect nothing less from her," she said. "Shannon is stubborn, but she's willing to accept your status as Head Witch until she has a chance to try again. The Henbanes, however, never had a chance at winning the title fairly."

"If you think Tiffany's the mastermind, how can I prove it?"

"With difficulty, I imagine." She looked over my shoulder. "*What* did you do to my accounts?"

"Nothing," I said. "These are mine. Besides, someone tried to kill me with a cursed pen, so I think I'm justified in switching to doing things the digital way for the foreseeable future."

She sniffed. "You're determined to stamp all over my legacy, aren't you?"

"You're welcome to take it up with Mum if you have an issue with how the coven is being run," I said. "The Head Witch is more of a ceremonial role, or so I'm told. Carmilla also told me that you fought your own battles back in the day."

"Did she now?" Grandma cast a disgruntled look at her

familiar. "That was a long time ago, and I was willing to accept the risks."

"So am I," I said. "I won't let anyone else place their lives on the line for my sake, especially if the Henbanes are still scheming to take my position by force."

Tiffany had yet to make a statement on her niece's actions, but Persephone was sitting in a jail cell, and Nolan and his rat wouldn't be getting off lightly for their role in the events. I expected Ramsey to ask me to come to the office and remove the spell I'd placed on the rat so he could stand trial at some point… but Tiffany wouldn't be facing punishment. She'd hidden her tracks well.

Grandma huffed. "Your funeral."

I could have reminded her that *her* funeral was still all too clear in my memory, but I didn't. "Thanks for understanding."

My phone buzzed with a message from Ramsey, asking me to drop by the police station. When I rose to my feet, Grandma tutted. "Skiving off already?"

"No, I'm going to undo the spell I put on one of the murderers," I said. "When I used the sceptre to cast a freeze-frame spell, it turned him into a statue. In rat form. Were you going to tell me that might happen?"

"Oh, that?" She cackled. "Delightful, isn't it? Don't try the rain spell indoors unless you want to use a boat to get around."

"I didn't plan to," I said. "How did you learn to use the sceptre when it first chose you? It's far stronger than a regular wand."

"Not to everyone." She gave me a considering look. "I suppose it *did* choose you as worthy."

"I'm not sure what you mean," I said. "The sceptre always picks its wielder. It chose me because I was there."

"That's what you think?" Grandma's ghost let out a cackle that made me scowl at her. "Oh, don't look so offended. The sceptre doesn't simply pick the first person who touches it."

"I know." But I'd thought the sceptre had deemed me worthy because I'd caught its predecessor's killer, not because I was the best Head Witch for the job.

"Then you should also know the sceptre is said to make its choice based on who it believes is the best Head Witch for this particular moment in time."

My mouth parted. "You mean the sceptre *did* choose me over Mum?"

"Yes, it did." She cackled again. "I bet that annoys her to no end, but she can't argue with the sceptre."

My phone buzzed again. "*You* tried to argue with it."

"I most certainly did not," she said. "You're the Head Witch, whether any of us likes it or not."

"Does that mean you're going to help me?" I asked. "I could use some pointers on using the sceptre."

"Don't push your luck," she said. "Go and see that brother of yours. Tell him not to make too much of a mess of my office."

"*My* office," I muttered, but I'd won a victory in getting her to admit the sceptre had chosen me over everyone else, including Mum. Grandma and I might not have seen eye to eye on a lot of things, but there was still a great deal she could teach me. If she was patient with me, I was more than willing to learn.

Upon arriving at the police station, I found myself ushered through to the holding cells at the back, where I used the spectre to undo my freeze-frame spell on the rat. After bouncing off the walls, the shifter fell into a heap, still in the form of a rat.

"If he thinks he'll get out of the trial if he stays in that form, he's wrong," said Ramsey. "He's due to be tried after Persephone Henbane."

"Has Tiffany said anything yet?" I asked.

"She's denied all connection with her niece's scheming," he said. "She refused to even come to the trial."

"Grandma is convinced that Persephone didn't come up with that scheme alone," I said. "I think she's right."

"Maybe, but there's no proof," he said. "We'll see how the trial goes. It'll take place tomorrow morning if you want to come."

"I'll be there." Even if Tiffany walked free, we'd have at least one Henbane witch incarcerated where she couldn't harm me. "Ah—what did you do with Minty and Jarvis?"

"I sent them home," he said. "Another contender offered to take care of them."

"At least they have each other."

That was a small consolation, but the two familiars hadn't been totally responsible for their owners' choices. Hopefully, the next person who took them in would have a better influence on them.

On the way back to my office, I dropped by the café to speak to Rowan and found her working behind the counter with Ralph perched on her shoulder.

"You got the job, then?"

"That's right." She smiled at me. "Sorry I didn't show

up to last night's trophy ceremony. I didn't know it would end up being that exciting."

"Honestly, you didn't miss much," I said. "Except Vanessa barging off in a huff because nobody was paying attention to her."

"She won, didn't she?"

"Yes, but everyone was more interested in learning about how I caught the killer," I said.

"I bet," she said. "I don't mind not winning, for the record, but I'm glad my sister didn't get the prestige she wanted."

"The contest isn't that much of a big deal," I said. "Though Anne and Malcolm raked in a fortune from bets on previous contests."

"I heard," she said. "Word says the Henbanes were involved in the murders, but that Persephone acted alone."

"I don't think she did, but it'll be difficult to prove when Tiffany is refusing to even come to the trial," I said. "The next contest isn't going to be for a while, which is good, because I think I'll be in charge of the next one."

"Can't you leave that to your assistant?"

"I might have to," I said. "I'm still learning what traditions I'm allowed to keep and which I'm not, but I think I'm making progress with Grandma."

"Does that mean she's going to give you some time off?" she asked. "For, say, a gaming session or *The Lord of the Rings* movie marathon in my new flat above the café?"

"If I'm free this weekend, I'd love to, but I still need to rat-proof my office." The smell of coffee reminded me why I'd come here. "Anyway, I'd like a latte, please."

Rowan went to fetch my drink, while I looked towards

the door in case any of my family's familiars showed up. Or Harvey.

Instead, Piper walked in. She put on a frosty expression when she saw Rowan giving me my drink, but she came over to the counter. "Hey, Robin. I didn't know you'd have any free time today."

"I'm supposed to be on my way back to the office from the police station," I explained. "Dropped by here to grab a latte."

"Good choice," she said. "Rowan, I'll have one of the same."

Rowan gave her a confused stare, but she remained in barista mode. "One minute."

"Are you trying to show her you forgive her?" I asked in an undertone when Rowan went to get her drink.

"Maybe." Piper looked embarrassed. "I was going to wait for her to apologise to *me* for accusing my familiar of attacking hers, but I did treat her kind of badly after she did that interview with the press. Besides, I don't like fighting with people."

"Hey, if it means I can invite both of you to meet up at the Fox's Den, then I'm all for it," I said. "Oh, by the way, I saw Harvey last night. At the ceremony."

"He came to the ceremony?" she asked. "I guess you did get your date. Kind of."

"Not what I planned, but I'll take it."

I could be Head Witch and still have a life at the same time. Someday, I might even have time to use my new camera. I could dream.

After fetching my coffee, I walked back to the office in good spirits, which swiftly faded when I found none other than Aunt Shannon waiting outside my door. At least she hadn't tried to get into my office, though I'd kept the invisible ink on the door in case she got any ideas about planting more sage on the property.

"Can I help you?" I asked. "How's Vanessa?"

"Fine," she said. "If you expect her to be happy that you stole her win, then you're mistaken."

"I didn't steal anything. She has a shiny trophy now." It wasn't my fault nobody cared about her victory. "Is there something I can do for you? If you have any issues you want to raise, then you're welcome to bring them up at this afternoon's meeting. I trust you'll show up on time."

Her jaw twitched. "Actually, I wanted a word with my mother."

"Grandma?" Was she joking? "You want to talk to her?"

"Yes, I do," she said.

"So you're not going to admit to leaving sage by the door?" When she simply glowered at me, I said, "I can look for Grandma, but I can't promise she'll want to talk to you."

Aunt Shannon looked me over. "You aren't the Head Witch I expected you to be."

"I'm choosing to take that as a compliment." I headed into my office and called for Grandma's ghost. "Grandma, Aunt Shannon is here to talk to you. If you want to question her about the sage, I'm sure it'll be fun to hear her excuses."

"This better be good." She drifted out of the office, while Tansy and I returned to my desk. I had a meeting to prepare for, plus Persephone's trial tomorrow. I added the latter to the calendar on my laptop while making a mental note to keep an eye on Tiffany. I didn't believe for a moment that this scheme would be her last.

"Everything okay, Head Witch?" asked Chloe.

"Sure." I rested the sceptre against the desk at my feet, always within reach. Whatever its reasons for choosing me as Head Witch, I needed to trust that it would reveal them to me in time.

Until then, I had work to do.

ABOUT THE AUTHOR

Elle Adams lives in the middle of England, where she spends most of her time reading an ever-growing mountain of books, planning her next adventure, or writing. Elle's books are humorous mysteries with a paranormal twist, packed with magical mayhem.

She also writes urban and contemporary fantasy novels as Emma L. Adams.

Visit http://www.elleadamsauthor.com/ to find out more about Elle's books.

www.ingramcontent.com/pod-product-compliance
Lightning Source LLC
Chambersburg PA
CBHW020808190726
48285CB00006B/2204